Once Upon A Weekend

stories by

A.C. Townsend

Published by Scratch Pad LLC.

ISBN-10:   0692952845
ISBN-13:   978-0692952849

Novels by A.C. Townsend

**The Trinity Conspiracy
series**

Journey of The Dead
Trinity Road
The Path Home

Destinations

Each Day Is An Adventure

Each day is an adventure
What treasures wait this morn?
Some call out, some are silent
Some ecstatic, some forlorn.

Some are eager to be noticed
Others hope just to be found
One brief glance with open eyes
Will see them all around.

Each day is a new volume
Stories breathless to rejoice
Boundless in their telling
They only need a voice.

Resident or passerby
To idle or employ
Each day is an adventure
To discover and enjoy.

The Legend of Laura Lake

The ancient roadbed parallels the length of town, disappears into the undergrowth as it approaches the old farmhouse, and emerges beyond the barn as a narrow footpath descending to the lakeshore. Across the lake linger the decaying ruins of the school, captive to four walls that guard its boundaries, twice destroyed by fire over the course of two and a half centuries, and abandoned for longer than anyone remains alive to remember.

Time fractures the stone walls. Weather erodes the remains. Massive vines drop anchor in moss-lined crevices. It is said that one can sometimes hear the cry of an angry child or a chorus of voices from beyond the north wall. The south wall is a hunting ground for reptiles. The east wall lies broken by the wind. The west wall, indeed the whole western quarter of the campus, is a mystery. Some say unspeakable horrors were committed there under gnarled shadows of low-hanging trees. Others recall stories of a graveyard where acres of forgotten children are buried.

There are also rumors that when the moon is full, spirits of the deceased roam the corridors of the school and patrol the boundary walls, that the more daring wraiths breach the east wall to haunt the lakeshore, and that any person foolish enough to trespass through their memories will add another grave to those along the west wall.

"This can't be right."

Laura parked and climbed slowly out of her car, taking in her surroundings as she closed the door. Faded wood and stone buildings faced each other across a half mile of two-lane road before terminating into nothing. There wasn't another vehicle in sight.

"What is this place – a ghost town?" she muttered.

A small boy gaped at her red convertible from around the corner of the nearest building.

She smiled. "Hi, there!"

The boy turned and fled.

Laura drew a determined breath. Her cream-colored dress and five-inch heels set her glaringly apart from the dust-and-denim locals who gawked as she mounted the rickety steps of the old country store. They straggled through the door in her wake, congregating in a corner as those heels clipped a march straight to the cash register.

The aging proprietor stared at Laura across the worn counter. He focused briefly on the crimson dahlia that adorned her hat, followed a cascade of golden waves to her shoulders, and swept a glance across her direct, blue-eyed gaze before finally offering the greeting he knew she needed to hear.

"Can I help you?"

"I certainly hope so," she said. "I was on my way to Malison, but somehow I got lost."

One of their observers dropped a can of soda. The can's rhythmic roll across the plank floor and the customer's hurried steps as he chased it down were the only sounds in the store. Beads of sweat appeared on the man's forehead as he retrieved the can and held it close. He glanced nervously at Laura.

Laura deigned him a look down her uplifted nose before turning back to the proprietor.

"It's obvious you aren't accustomed to receiving visitors here," she said, "so I won't trouble you any longer than necessary to ask directions."

"Oh, you'd be surprised." The old man quelled an itch in his left ear with a stiff pinky finger. "You'd be surprised how many people end up in Foundless."

Laura shook her head. "I haven't traveled very far. I've only been on the road for a couple of hours. But I've never heard of this place."

"Young lady, you've gone farther than you think." Knowing eyes met and held her gaze. "And in the wrong direction, at that."

A fly droned past Laura's face and bounced clumsily off the window.

"But you are on your way to Malison," he confirmed.

"That's what I said," Laura agreed impatiently. "But you're not making sense. I can't be on the right path if I'm headed the wrong direction, now can I?"

"You learn fast," he said. "Now that we've cleared that up, are you certain you want to continue on this road, or might it be wiser to choose another destination?"

She gave a short laugh. "I don't know what you're talking about, but I do know that I didn't come here for a sermon."

"You came here because you're lost." The old man smiled for the first time. "Directions and sermons have a lot in common. How did you get this far?" he asked gently. "Didn't you have instructions to follow before you started out? Somebody to tell you how to get where you are supposed to go?"

"Of course I did!" she snapped.

"So how did you end up in Foundless?"

"Not that it's any of your business, but I got a late start, so I decided to take a shortcut. That road didn't lead where I anticipated, and by the time I realized I was in unfamiliar territory, I had gone too far to turn back and start over."

"You're following the path of your own choosing. You're here because of the decisions you made."

"Thanks for pointing that out," Laura said sarcastically. "I'd just love to stay and continue this riveting dialogue, but I've already lost a lot of time, and if I don't reach my destination soon,

I risk losing my job."

"What job would that be?"

"If you must know, I am a teacher. I have assisted instructors in some of the most prestigious institutions of education in the country, and I am en route to my first full-time position at the elite private school of Malison."

The proprietor exchanged a grave look with the group of patrons gathered in the far corner of his store. He nodded at Laura. "Well, now we know what you're running to. What we need to address is what you're running from, and why."

"As I said, that's really none of your business." She exhaled in exasperation. "Can you tell me how to get there, or not?"

The old man studied her expression for an endless moment before conceding with a reluctant nod. He walked to the end of the counter and motioned for her to follow him out the door.

On the porch, he offered Laura a handshake.

"My name is Jason. Don't you forget that. If you need anything or find that you'd like to change your mind after all somewhere down the line, you ask for me. Okay?"

"Jason," she agreed. "Now for those directions!"

"On your way here, about a mile back, you passed a sign pointing toward Edgar Lake."

"I saw it. You might want to have that sign replaced," Laura said. "It's barely hanging onto the post by one nail, and the paint is so faded that the words are hardly legible."

"We're about to take care of that," Jason assured her. "Turn off the highway at the sign and follow the old road to the lake. The road is narrow, so drive carefully. When you reach the lakeshore, you'll see a graveled pull-off. That's where you'll park. You'll see your destination across the lake."

"Why am I parking on this side of the lake if –"

"A footbridge spans the east end of lake," Jason interrupted. "It's the only access to the school."

"That can't be true! There has to be a road to the property."

"Why is that?"

"Because this is a prestigious, private institution we're talking about! Malison promises the kind of success that most people only ever dream of! The salary for one year alone promises to be more than I could make elsewhere in a decade."

"Who made you those promises?" Jason wanted to know.

"Well, no one specific person," Laura retorted. "But the place has a glowing reputation."

"It would be wise to investigate the source of that glow," Jason advised.

The depth of Laura's sigh attested to the fragility of her patience.

"But, yes, you have to cross the footbridge and follow the path to the gate."

"Well, at least that part is right," Laura said. "The campus is walled for privacy. I remember hearing about that."

"They're expecting you."

"Actually, no, not really."

Jason looked her in the eye.

"I said I'm on my way to my first full-time position, and I am!" Laura asserted. "That's my goal, and I'm going to achieve it. I don't know how many positions are available at Malison, and I don't want to lose my chance at being accepted. They'll be glad to have me on their staff when they learn my history and see that I'm willing to do whatever is necessary to fit their standards."

The boy who had stared at Laura's car appeared beside Jason carrying an old metal lantern. Jason took it from him and held it out to Laura.

"It will be dark by the time you get there."

"I won't need that." Laura laughed. "Just sell me a flashlight and a couple of batteries."

"A can of kerosene and a box of matches will last longer," Jason said. "Lee will get you a flashlight. But take the lantern anyway."

Laura rolled her eyes.

"Humor me," Jason said. "Pretend you believe I know what I'm talking about."

The little boy handed Laura a plastic pink flashlight with two batteries in a blister pack. He held onto the package until Laura looked down at him.

"Miss Laura?"

"Yes, Lee?"

"Beware trespassing Edgar Lake."

Laura flinched at the child's solemn warning, unnerved by the intensity in his beseeching eyes.

"Thank you, Lee!" Jason said. He smiled at Laura. "No charge."

"Thank you, Jason and Lee," Laura said with exaggerated patience.

She descended the steps to her car and got in, placing the lantern and the flashlight in the passenger seat.

"Goodbye, Laura," Jason whispered into the dusk.

Laura glanced over her shoulder as she waved goodbye to Jason, startled to see the crowd of somber faces, twice the number of patrons from inside the store, who stared grimly after her as she drove out of sight.

Laura sped right past the sign after swearing she wouldn't, and miles elapsed before a narrow lane presented an opportunity to turn around and retrace her path. She almost missed the road again in the darkness, her headlights flashing across the decrepit sign just in time for her to veer off the highway and plunge into the narrow, tree-lined corridor that promised to conclude at Edgar Lake.

Jason's questions lingered in her thoughts, awaiting answers she was neither willing nor able to give. He offered solid advice. She repaid his concern with sarcasm. He treated her kindly despite her condescending attitude, as if he recognized truths about her that she herself failed – or refused – to see. And he had never even met her before.

Her confidence lost its abrasive edge. There was still time to turn back. She could change her mind, and no one would ever have to know how close she had come to following through on her rash decision. Subconsciously, she knew she was making wrong choices for wrong reasons. But she was tired of trying and failing. This time she would get what she wanted, regardless of the cost. If she could force fate to bend to her will, she would never have to admit she had been wrong. Not even to herself.

Laura turned on the radio to dispel the shadows gathering in her mind. Static spewed from the speakers. The deafening hiss intensified her sense of foreboding. She switched it off and began talking to herself in an attempt to ignore the instinct that set her nerves on edge, screaming warnings of unnamed dangers that couldn't possibly exist. She shook her head at herself for being silly.

"Jason wasn't joking; this is a narrow road," she said. "He didn't tell me it's only one lane. I hope I don't meet anyone coming from the other direction. There isn't room for two cars to pass!"

The unfamiliar taunted her perceptions in the darkness. She would have sworn no road existed at all, but that foliage retreated and pavement generated in obedience to the glow of her car's headlights advancing into the undergrowth.

"I should have asked him about the distance from Foundless to the lake. And how long the walk will be around the lake and over the bridge to Malison."

The radio abruptly spewed static again, and Laura gave a sharp cry as she smacked the button to turn it off.

"Okay," she told herself. "It's okay. Just drive."

The trembling of her voice did nothing to calm her fears.

Night thickened into a solid drape through which oxygen no longer flowed. Trees closed around the car with the claustrophobic presence of a living tribe seeking to absorb Laura into their own flesh for nourishment, for perverse pleasure. She heard the thrum of voices luring her mind, dragging her name through the sizzle of static from her radio.

Laura cried out again and stomped the accelerator to the floor. The car erupted from the woods onto a lane that bordered an open field. She sped alongside a row of mummified fence posts sporadically connected by crumbling gray boards. Laura smacked the radio into silence once more and stared into the blackness that receded through her rearview mirror. Nothing pursued her from the woods.

"No *thing?*" she said aloud, and laughed as her voice cracked with fear. "Laura, you need a hot bath and a good night's sleep. Since when do you allow your imagination to run away with you like that?"

She slowed to a reasonable speed as she followed two dirt wheel tracks separated by a strip of tall green grass that swept the underside of her car.

"I don't understand this," she said. "The road to Malison has to be smooth and well-maintained. And wide! Based on reputation alone, the place stays notoriously busy. Traffic in and out must be constant. I turned off at the sign for Edgar Lake like Jason said to do. Surely he wouldn't have sent me out here as a joke."

A long-abandoned farmhouse rose from the waist-high grass on her left. Shards of glass clung to second-story window frames, reflecting moonlight like eyes glinting from the depths of a grieving soul. Laura took in the sagging porch, collapsing roof, and the broken rocking chair just inside the gaping front door and experienced a pang of sorrow for the loss of a once-happy life.

A quarter mile farther, as she rolled past the fallen remnants of a barn, she caught her first glimpse of moonlight on Edgar Lake.

"I hope someone is still awake at the school," Laura said, "someone who is willing and available to answer the door. I should have asked in town about a place to spend the night. Then I could have driven out in the morning when the day was off to a fresh start, instead of showing up at a time when most people are going to bed."

Mist hovered across the surface of the lake, wafting ashore to meet Laura as her car coasted to a stop in the graveled pull-off. Fog shifted among long-neglected trees in the adjacent orchard as if bringing them to life, and Laura shuddered at the illusion of grotesque, multi-limbed figures marching in slow motion to the music of the night – frog and cricket song, haunting cries of birds whose species she could not recall.

And laughter. Laughter from across Edgar Lake.

The clear plastic encasing the pink flashlight had been opened, making it easy for Laura to rip out the flashlight and quickly insert the batteries. She switched on a feeble beam that barely lit her feet through the thick fog.

Laura retrieved the lantern from her car and struck a match to light it. The warm, golden glow immediately gave her confidence. Darkness retreated from her footsteps, and the mist swirled reluctantly back to the lakeshore.

She pulled her suitcase from the back seat. The trunk of her car held two cardboard boxes filled with additional clothing and the few possessions she had not wanted to leave behind. Those boxes could wait, she decided, until morning. She couldn't carry everything by herself. Perhaps an escort from the school could return with her tomorrow to collect the rest of her things.

"Now to find that footbridge," she resolved.

Laura set out to her right, leaving the farm and the orchard behind. She stumbled along a safe distance from the water's edge, wishing she had dressed for a cross-country hike instead of for a job interview at an elite educational institution. The slender heels that appeared so pretty and professional when she dressed at midday now caused her to twist her ankles and lose her balance.

"This doesn't make sense," she protested under her breath. "No highway, no parking lot. No sign directing people to the school. Not even a path to follow from the pull-off to the bridge. How on earth do students and staff get to Malison? How are food and supplies transported to the school? What happens when an emergency requires an ambulance or the fire department to reach the campus?"

And no lights from across the lake. The full moon penetrated the fog to illuminate what appeared to be jagged remains of a long-forgotten nightmare, black and silent but for one moment of childish laughter that echoed hollow and lonely from beyond the walls that encaged her dreams.

For the first time, Laura questioned the breathtaking assumptions that had influenced her decision to pursue a new life at Malison. Eager anticipation and urgency to escape the failures of her past made for little planning and less confirmation. She simply assumed that her expectations would prove true. So far, every shred of evidence attested that she was wrong. Dead wrong.

"Circumstantial evidence," she insisted aloud. "Heresay from people who are jealous that they don't have the courage to do what I'm doing. That's all it is. Just wait till I get there. I'll show *them!*"

Them who had told her she was making a huge mistake; them who asked, begged, ordered her not to go. Them who loved her and them who barely knew her. Them who were younger but wiser, and them who had decades more experience along the journey of Life. Them who urged her to think about, learn about, pray about what she was about to do.

Prayer had not occurred to her since she was a child. God, Laura knew in her heart, did not bless endeavors that flew in the face of His word and His will. Such endeavors included her impetuous resolve to take her chances on Malison.

She waded through a stretch of low-growing briars that clutched at her ankles. Damp webs and whining insects skittered across her face. She wanted to kick off her shoes and run for her life, but she was afraid to place her bare feet on the ground.

The better part of an hour had passed by the time Laura came to the footbridge. According to Jason, she should be within a thousand feet of the gate in the east wall once she walked across. The moon faded to a reddish haze, frightening her enough to murmur a prayer that the blood on the moon might not be hers.

Laura held her lantern high and stepped up onto the first wooden plank.

Lights abruptly flooded the grounds across Edgar Lake.

Malison had awakened.

Laura stood motionless in the center of the bridge, too frightened to proceed, too ashamed to turn back. She knew beyond the shadow of a doubt that she was about to commit a deliberate wrong that would affect her life in ways she could not begin to imagine. The unknown variable claimed her decision. She already knew what she was leaving behind, and she was desperate for a bright and beautiful change, even if she had to wring it from the dregs of the blackest sin.

"There's no reason to be afraid," Laura said, still seeking comfort in the sound of her own voice. "Remember why you came. Think of all the wonderful details you've heard about this place."

They were silent now, those voices that urged, cajoled, insisted she go there. Ignore advice to the contrary, they said. Your intuition is lying. Don't worry about consequences. Don't listen to warnings. They belittled her fears. Ridiculed her hesitation. Mocked her questions, but provided no answers. Convinced her she would be missing out on the most incredible opportunity of her life if she turned her back on Malison.

And now the stories she had chosen to believe amounted to nothing more than cruel delusions: colorful, enticing, too good to be true.

"So I've pursued speculations instead of specifics," Laura said. "But doesn't everybody? You can't be certain you want to go to a place you've never been, no matter how much you've heard about it."

She picked up her suitcase and held the lantern a little higher.

"I'll just go and see what it's like. If I find that I can't handle it, if anything about the situation makes me uncomfortable, I can change my mind and leave."

Laura continued toward her destination as quickly as her aching feet would allow, but something happened the moment she stepped off the bridge.

The decision was complete. She could feel it. She couldn't turn back now even if she wanted to.

Malison wouldn't allow it.

Laura trembled, overcome with terror at having walked into a trap laid just for her.

No, her heart cried. *I'm in charge. I'm in control. This is my life, and I call the shots!*

Even as the objections crossed her mind, she realized control was merely an illusion. A mortally dangerous illusion. Laura had insisted on getting her way, and she had won the right to lose.

And lost she was. So very lost.

But she was also relieved.

Regardless of her dread of what lay in wait, despite vines of possession already ensnaring her heart, a soothing thought caressed Laura's mind: the burden of choice was no longer hers to carry. In its place, something comforting and sinister awoke inside her, a vise compressing her soul, subjugating her spirit, mind, and body to an indwelling companion who assumed immediate and absolute authority.

The path of least resistance curved away from the bridge. Each flat stone surface was etched with symbols and laid alongside others in designs that appeared to reflect the constellations overhead.

"Heaven on Earth." Laura studied the stones as she walked the path. "Think positive. Despite all of the problems I've had today, I'm almost there. I've made it. Everything will be just fine once I'm inside with other people. Right now I'm tired, and fear and unfamiliarity are causing me to see and hear strange and illogical things that simply do not exist."

A pair of misshapen gargoyles snarled at Laura from atop massive stone pillars as she approached the east wall. She shrank from their malignant stares as she hurried underneath them.

"They aren't real," she chided herself.

The creatures watched her steps slow as she stared in disbelief at the enormous iron gates set into the east wall. Thick gray vines, armored with thorns, grew from each pillar and twined into elaborate branches that converged at the ancient lock that married the two with one iron ring. A knocker, Laura realized, and wondered again if she were too late for anyone to hear.

A viper, Laura realized, and her hand paused short of grasping the braided coils crowned with a triangular head that regarded her through venomous emerald eyes.

Everything in her screamed for escape. *Run!* But she had ventured too deep into Malison. She had invited Malison into her soul, and Malison had claimed her offering. Her new master, so recently acquired, would hurt her if she attempted to renege on her commitment to become what Malison intended her to be.

"Welcome, Laura."

The voice knifed through the fog and the fear as it slid into Laura's heart, smooth as hot steel.

A key turned in a lock, a latch clicked, and the left gate swung inward to reveal the speaker.

If Snow White matured into the Wicked Queen, Laura thought, this is exactly what she would become: tall and slim with alabaster skin, scarlet lips, raven hair, eyes the same hypnotic poison as those of the serpent on the gate – and older, much older than the damsel who fled her father's palace, took refuge among dwarves, and stole the heart of a handsome prince.

This stranger knew her name. Laura's fear escalated once more.

"Don't be afraid, my dear." The woman attempted a smile, but her face would not conform to the command. The resulting grimace made Laura's blood run cold.

The woman lifted her arm in a graceful gesture and beckoned for Laura to enter.

"I am Thana, headmistress of the world within these walls. Welcome, Laura, to Malison!"

The gate swung closed. Laura looked back, startled to find herself inside the grounds when she had not been aware of stepping across the threshold.

"We've anticipated your arrival and are pleased that you followed through with your intentions." Thana touched icy fingertips to the back of Laura's arm, and together the women followed the stone path that led from the bridge all the way into the heart of the campus.

"Some people do change their minds, you know," Thana continued. "Oh, not as many as once did. Your world is so full of distractions that people don't think anymore. When they don't think, they're easy to beguile. Like you were, my dear."

Laura saw that grimace again.

"Deception is so much easier when people aren't paying attention," Thana said. "Enrollment at Malison is at an all-time high, and I don't believe we will ever see another drop in attendance. New people arrive constantly."

"How?" Laura demanded. "I barely found my way here, and I didn't meet anyone else on their way in or out."

"The path is different for everyone, but the destination is always the same. And once you have arrived, your residency is permanent." Thana laughed a series of hollow syllables. "You can walk away, of course, and eventually you will try. You can change locations as many times as you like in the years to come. You might leave Malison, but Malison will never leave you."

"I don't know what you're talking about." Laura stopped and looked back, but the gate, the wall, and the path behind her were memories in the mist. "But I do feel that I have been deceived. Where is the beautiful campus? The luxurious rooms? The elite environment? This place is supposed to be nearly perfect, but what I've experienced so far could rival a horror flick."

"Your questions will be answered in due time," Thana reassured her. "For now, I'll show you to your suite, and you can get settled in. You are tired and hungry and not at all sure about your decision to come here."

"You assume a lot," Laura said. Her response was curt with resentment. Fear unassuaged had progressed to anger.

"Not assumption, but experience," Thana said. "I have been headmistress for more years than you have been alive. Before that, I was a teacher. Before that, I was a student. And before that, I was just as lost as you, a soul in need of solace, desperately seeking direction, but finding no compass that could locate a path I wished to follow."

"Until you found Malison," Laura supplied.

"Until Malison found me," Thana said. "And here we are! Perhaps your chosen destiny will meet your expectations after all."

They emerged from the fog as though stepping through a wall, and Laura gasped at a scene straight out of her most extravagant imagination.

Palatial stone buildings, some two centuries old, spread across the campus. Rising from two to six stories, each window brilliant with lamplight, they promised in an instant to bring Laura's fantasies to life.

She stood in awe of their presence until Thana took her by the hand.

"The residence halls are this way," she said, and Laura allowed herself to be led along the stone path between the first two structures and into the labyrinth that was Malison.

In her dreams, Laura roamed the ruins of Malison. Crumbled walls overtaken with moss and ivy intruded into her path. A pair of large rats chewing carrion on a stone ledge followed her progress with moonlit eyes. It was gone, all of it, the vast campus reduced to the remains of five much smaller structures than those she had toured upon her arrival.

And it had been gone for a very, very long time.

Dense weeds, hip-high, concealed rancid clots of rotting vegetation, slimy and wet with the stench of decay, that squished underfoot as she set out across a field toward the west wall. The weeds lashed her bare legs, and she realized she was still wearing the dress in which she had arrived, though flat slippers replaced the five-inch heels she had previously worn. The slippers immediately filled with putrid muck as she pushed toward her unknown destination.

A pair of white-haired children stood on the far side of the field awaiting her arrival. She tried to hurry to them, but could only trudge along in place. The sensation left her exhausted. She stood before them without warning, without having crossed the field, and now she wore a black dress and a black hat with a narrow mesh veil.

She smiled at the ghostly children. Their faces contorted in agony as they attempted to form smiles in return, and the little boy stuttered a monosyllabic 'ha-ha-ha,' and the little girl threw back her head and wailed.

Laura thrashed awake, panting in terror as she scrambled for the lamp on her bedside table. She clicked it on and gave a little scream.

Reclining in the chair beside her bed, holding an open book as though he had been reading in the pitch darkness, sat Jason.

"What," Laura managed. She sat up, rubbed her eyes, and tried again. "How did you get into my room?"

Jason straightened a satin ribbon between the pages and closed his book. "I just wanted to remind you, Laura. To call my name if you need me." He smiled.

She frowned. "I didn't call your name. I don't need you. I just had a nightmare, that's all."

"Perhaps," Jason said. "Or not. People are notorious for choosing to see what they want to see instead of what is really there."

"Another sermon, so soon?" Laura's condescending sarcasm startled even herself.

Jason removed his reading glasses and leaned forward. "Tell me, Laura, which is the deception, and which is the truth. Are you sitting here talking to me, or are you lost among the ruins of your life?"

Darkness swallowed her in an instant, and she stood ankle-deep in wet grass, gazing across endless rows of gravestones smoothed by decades of rain and snow and sun and fingertips that gradually erased the identities of the countless corpses long since vacated by suddenly-freed souls.

The white-haired children stood at the cemetery's edge. The little girl reached for her hand.

Laura stumbled backward and found herself sitting on the edge of her bed, staring at Jason.

"You might want to wash the mud off your feet before you lie down," he suggested, and was gone.

Laura stretched luxuriously. She had slept reasonably well following her dual nightmares involving Jason and those strange children. She frowned thoughtfully. She had turned off the lamp when she went to bed. If her encounters occurred only in her mind, why was the lamp on right now?

For that matter, why was it still black outside? Laura felt as though she had overslept, yet morning must still be hours away. She reached for her alarm clock. The digital display blinked a row of zeros.

She got out of bed anyway, and showered, and dressed, and applied a touch of makeup. Laura decided to explore the campus as she awaited sunrise. She peered out her second-story window and smiled when she saw people skirting pools of lamplight on the sidewalks. Her joy faded as she observed the shadowed grounds below. People sat on benches, leaned against walls, stood in silent clusters, all lingering, but without apparent purpose.

Laura retrieved her pink flashlight from her bag and locked the door to her quarters with a vintage brass key.

The atmosphere clung stale and humid and, as far as Laura could tell, Malison was devoid of life. The people she had watched from her window had vanished. The beautiful campus stretched before her, making her laugh at her fears. She walked slowly, admiring facades of buildings she had no desire to enter. It was enough that she could remain here among them.

She rounded a corner and almost bumped into a man who leaned against a garden wall picking a string, only one string, of the guitar strapped loosely around his shoulders.

"Excuse me!" Laura sidestepped the man. "Are you an

instructor here? My name is Laura. I have an interview tomorrow morning. I hope to secure a teaching position."

The man's hands went still against the guitar. He closed his eyes as if in pain before turning his head just enough to peer at Laura through strands of graying, shoulder-length hair.

"There is no tomorrow," he said.

Laura recoiled from the hopelessness that marred the man's lined and weathered face.

Plink, plink, plink, he played, the same lifeless note on the same out-of-tune string.

The man turned to Laura, confusion in his eyes. "It won't talk to me. Why won't it talk to me?" His tone became desperate, and his shoulders heaved with tremendous sobs, but no tears fell from his eyes. "What have I done?" he cried. *"What have I done!"* he roared, yanking the strap over his head. He raised the guitar high and slammed it against the garden wall.

Laura fled down the sidewalk toward a silent rectangle of light flooding through a pair of open doors. She ducked inside and winced at the sudden blare of music throbbing from a band on a distant stage. The expansive floor was packed with people, from teenagers to elderly men and women. They danced and gyrated. Threw their hands in the air and screamed. Stood and vibrated with seizures. Jerked awkwardly from side to side with empty expressions on their faces, unaware of their surroundings.

Laura hugged the wall as she navigated the perimeter of the auditorium, scanning the horde for Thana. But Thana wouldn't be here, she thought. This wasn't the sort of entertainment a woman of Thana's distinction would indulge. On the far side, she came upon a wet bar and vending area. The counter and tables were clogged with people openly partaking of illegal drugs. Some drifted behind vacant stares, focused on a world only they could see. Others screamed – in horror, anger, ecstasy – or laughed as though life were an absolute joke. A couple in the corner fell to the floor in convulsions, retching and foaming at the mouth, twitching as though hooked to an invisible electrical source, until at last they stopped moving, stopped breathing, stopped living.

In tears, Laura backed slowly away. She reversed her direction and headed for the door. From the stage, the lead guitarist incited his audience, encouraged them to party on, continued to play one solitary note, morphing one song into another. His voice felt oddly familiar. Laura stopped to study his face. Recognition left her weak.

The tortured musician who had just demolished his guitar against a stone wall now stood before an impressionable audience, having the time of his life, playing that same solitary note as though through it, he had achieved perfection. He laughed, sang a few words, shouted again to his fans.

Cringing against the wall, Laura hurried through the doors and out into the oppressive silence. Standing on the sidewalk just across the threshold, she watched the teeming throng as though viewing a muted movie. The music and noise were available only to those who entered in.

Laura retraced her steps to the garden wall and stared at the musician. He lay in the crevice where the wall met the ground, pulverizing pieces of the mutilated guitar with his fists as he grieved, raged, despaired in his own personal hell.

Laura turned away from the human wreckage and jogged to the nearest intersecting pathway. She walked between two buildings along a path she hadn't previously explored, looking for a friendly face, looking for morning. Another door invited her to enter, a single door spilling cool lamplight through a narrow glass pane.

Laura stepped inside the foyer of a residential hall much like her own. Doors stood open on both sides of the hall, and Laura heard the musician's despair in a multitude of female voices. She ventured forward and peered cautiously into the first room.

A woman stood before a dresser. The top was strewn with a variety of makeup, all of which had been applied liberally to the woman's face. Clothing and shoes cluttered the floor, and the woman yanked a brush viciously through her hair as she cursed her maker for not making her perfect. Laura recognized her. She continued on to the next room, and the next, pausing to look into each one as she hurried along the hall. An endless multitude of women of all ages, of all shapes, sizes, and complexions, mourned their imperfections.

But Laura had seen these women, just moments ago, dancing and laughing and flirting and drinking among countless friends in a noisy arena, celebrating their flawless lives.

Escaping once more out onto the sidewalk, Laura realized she had lost her way. She called out for Thana, but her voice evaporated into the stifling atmosphere.

"I'm still sleeping," Laura reassured herself. "That is the only way any of this could possibly make sense. I'll wake up in a little while, and I'll laugh about my crazy adventures while I get ready to meet Thana and the Board of Directors for my interview."

She stood tall and walked with more confidence than she possessed. She circled one building and then another, disconcerted by her surroundings. Though the landscape appeared normal, the buildings rose around her in a different layout than she recalled. She stopped and searched for something familiar, anything to guide her back the way she had come.

"Laura! There you are. We've been waiting for you, dear."

Laura flinched as Thana's icy fingertips touched the back of her arm.

"I know you haven't had time to create a lesson plan, so I've borrowed the first two chapters from another instructor for you to use. You'll be teaching college freshmen, which should be interesting, especially since you aren't much older than most of your students. I'll introduce you to your class." Thana walked away, but stopped when she saw that Laura wasn't following her.

"But I'm not even awake," Laura objected. "None of this is real."

"Malison is as real as you make it." Thana's thin, white face turned cadaverous in the moonlight.

Laura shuddered and felt herself giving in to fear.

"Okay, so what if this, right now, really is happening. It's still nonsense. I haven't even had my interview," Laura reminded her. "And the only reason I'm out here at this hour is because I couldn't sleep. Tomorrow morning, everything will be okay."

"There is no tomorrow," Thana said smoothly. "There is no morning. Oh, don't be frightened, my dear. You'll come to welcome the darkness. Soon it will be the only life you know."

Tears came before Laura could stop them. Terror thinned her voice to a high-pitched thread.

"I want to go home," she begged. "Just show me the way to the gate. I can make it back to my car on my own."

Even as she spoke, Laura gasped in awareness of her new master stirring inside her, exercising its authority, refusing to release its latest acquisition, calming and threatening and enticing and hurting her until she bowed her head in submission to its possession.

"There, you see?" Thana grimaced. "You're learning already! It's easy to live for the moment when you aren't distracted by thoughts of a future that doesn't exist."

"But I do have a future!" Laura cried. "That's why I came here – to achieve my goals and to show everybody that I can succeed, I can make this work, I can be who I want to be!"

"Your determination was obvious to us long before you arrived." Thana took Laura by the arm and steered her along the sidewalk. "That is why the Board decided to bypass the interview process. Your attitude as well as your aptitude secured your position in Malison."

"But this is all wrong," Laura said. "I was lured here by false pretenses. Malison isn't at all what it was made out to be. It is a lie. It is a broken promise. And I want to go home, now!"

Laura winced at the compression of her spirit by a massive, brutal hand.

"Let's compromise," Thana coaxed. "Give Malison a chance. You've only just arrived. Everything is unfamiliar, and nothing is more frightening than the unknown. Stay long enough to become acclimated – one week should suffice – and then if you are as determined to leave as you were to come here, you can go."

Laura slowed as they passed yet another cluster of people standing motionless and silent with far-away expressions.

"What is wrong with them?" Laura asked, putting Thana's offer on hold. "I've seen so many like them. They just stand outside the buildings as though they're waiting for the doors to open."

Thana stopped and offered Laura a handkerchief. "They stand by the doors to their dreams," she said. "Some people treat their ambitions as goals, and accomplish each one until their doors open. But they stop at the threshold and refuse to enter. Sometimes the dreamers don't want their doors to open, and so they never do."

Laura pressed the cloth to her eyes, absorbing the flow of tears. "No one would refuse the gift of their dreams coming true," she retorted.

"But that's the thing about dreams," Thana said. "When they come true, they aren't dreams anymore. It's easy to dream. Dreams are an escape from reality. When they come true, they *are* reality, with all the pressure and stress that comes with suddenly having everything you always wanted. Stewardship is a tremendous responsibility, especially when you are tending the desires of your heart. Wanting can be so much easier than having. That is the paradox of dreams."

"So all of these people's lives are on hold until they decide whether or not they want to realize the aspirations they've sacrificed everything to achieve?"

"As is yours, my dear." Thana nudged Laura's shoulder, and they continued across the campus. "Hope deferred makes the heart sick," she said proudly. "There is nothing more effective than disappointment to silence a soul."

"One week." Laura trembled with uncertainty.

"One week." Thana nodded.

"And then I can go home."

"If you can bear to leave." Thana stopped in the middle of a vast courtyard. She pointed to a structure rising from the shadows, at one solitary illuminated window. "Room 616. Your lesson plans are on your desk. Your students are awaiting your arrival."

"I'm not prepared to teach a class! You haven't even told me what subject you want me to teach, or how to teach it!"

"This is why you came, is it not?" Thana glared at Laura. "Your door is open. I will be terribly disappointed if you refuse to take advantage of this opportunity."

Laura gazed up at the window, watching the light grow dimmer the longer she stood and stared. She turned desperate eyes on Thana, but found herself alone.

The light flickered like candle flame guttering in a breeze. Laura rubbed her eyes with the handkerchief and made her decision. She would find her way inside the building and locate her classroom. She would talk to the students. She would glance through the materials Thana had placed on her desk and figure out what information Thana wanted her to share with them.

But when she opened her eyes, she stood before the residence hall in which she now lived. Frightened, angry, relieved, Laura flung open the door and ran all the way to her room.

Holding her lantern high, she followed the white-haired children among rows of gravestones. They held hands and spoke to each other in syllables she did not recognize. They glanced back often, ensuring she stayed with them.

At least the ground was solid this time. Laura looked down and saw that her black shoes were coated with white dust, like ashes. Across and down, across and down, she walked until she grew weary. She followed the children through a grove of trees and stopped, startled to see the ruins of Malison ahead in the moonlight. She realized she was returning from the West wall, though she could not remember having been there.

The children continued their zig-zag course toward the front of the cemetery. Here lay the most recently deceased below white headstones less eroded by nature and time.

They stopped in the first row. The boy stood on the left side of a new stone, the girl on the right, their clasped hands swinging back and forth above the name of the interred.

Laura knelt and held her lantern close to read the information they wanted her to see.

His name was Edgar Bohannon. The children's hands shadowed the date of his birth. But the date that he died was the day Laura crossed the bridge into Malison.

Tearing her way out of the cemetery with a scream, Laura leaped out of bed and reached for the lamp. "Jas – !" she stammered, and froze before the figure sitting in her chair.

"Expecting someone?" Thana asked.

Laura swallowed hard. "Why are you here?"

"You cried out in your sleep. I came to check on you. Now that you are awake, I'll be on my way." Thana paused by the door. "When you've had enough rest, come downstairs prepared to teach your first class."

"But you haven't told me who or what – "

"Whatever you imagine your career to be, my dear." Thana pulled the door closed, leaving Laura alone.

Except she wasn't alone.

Jason stood beside her. "Hello, Laura." He smiled.

Laura broke down and sobbed.

"This isn't how it's supposed to be!" Laura kicked off her dusty shoes and sat on the bed. She covered her face with her hands and wept. "Everything about this place is horrible!"

"And yet you are determined to stay." Jason pushed a box of tissues across the table.

"I can't fail again. I just can't," Laura insisted.

"Perhaps you are seeking success in the wrong place," Jason suggested. "It is all too easy to impose one's determination onto a situation. Our imagination can fabricate circumstances that really do exist only in our minds."

"No." Laura shook her head. "No, I'm not. I want to succeed as a teacher, and I'll do whatever it takes to achieve that objective."

"Like attend college, commit time to study, work hard to complete your assignments, and maintain a high grade point average? But that's boring, isn't it, when you could be cutting classes to date a married professor. Or like admitting to your parents that you were expelled from college because you used your tuition money to make a down payment on a car?"

"No one knows those things about me!" Laura shouted.

"You failed at college because you didn't want to be there, and you were angry at your parents for insisting that you go. You fail at relationships because you are afraid to share your heart with someone who is available to make a commitment. You've bluffed your way through life, and now you are desperate to force Malison to give you what you haven't put the effort into achieving in an honorable way. Everyone knows those things about you, Laura. The only person you're fooling is yourself."

"Everybody keeps telling me the right way to do things. That's okay for you and for them. But only I know what's right for me." Pride vanquished Laura's tears, and she sat up straight and tall.

"Laura, you aren't the first or the only person to experience paralyzing indecision about your future," Jason said gently. "You aren't the first person to think you know more than those who are offering instruction born of their own wisdom and experience. But there is no shame in learning from other people's mistakes. Maturity grows from admitting you were wrong, apologizing to people you've hurt, and taking responsibility for your actions."

"But I'm not wrong. If anybody got their feelings hurt, it's because they stuck their nose in my business. And I am taking responsibility for myself by pursuing my future my way." Laura swiped her nose with a tissue and stood. "Now if you will excuse me, I have a class to teach." She looked toward the window. "Even if it is the middle of the night."

"It is always night in Malison," Jason said. "Light is not welcome here."

"Whatever I imagine my career to be." Laura repeated Thana's words as soon as Jason walked out the door. "Well, I never wanted to work with college students. I planned to teach children about the age of that boy and girl who keep showing up in my nightmares."

She hadn't invested much time in her own education, but she was confident she could structure a lesson plan, and she felt she understood the psychological perspectives and learning abilities of children in the age range she wanted to teach.

"One thing at a time," she said. "I'll tell Thana I want to teach children. Once we've established who I'm going to teach, we'll decide what I'm going to teach them and how those lessons will be presented."

Laura showered, slipped into a dress, curled her hair, and applied makeup and perfume. In her imagination, she always saw herself dressed up and beautiful, standing in front of a classroom filled with adoring children who loved and worshipped her. She studied her reflection and added a jeweled clip to her hair.

"Just right," she said. She stepped into her five-inch heels and tried to smile as she left her room to meet Thana.

Little eyes stared at Laura from behind little desks in perfectly aligned rows. Little hands held little pencils, and each little face held the tension of hoping the new teacher would be kind.

Laura tried to smile at them and found that she couldn't. Her face resisted the effort.

Her master writhed within her spirit. Thus far it had been satisfied to hurt her only when she wanted to leave Malison. Now it communicated its intention to accomplish dire purposes through her.

Laura tried to keep her voice light so the children would not perceive the struggle within. "I am Miss Laura. Let's get acquainted, shall we? Raise your hand when I call your name."

She focused on maintaining a positive atmosphere, on earning the trust of her children, on setting a good example for them and noting what strengths and weaknesses were readily apparent in each of her students.

But the harder she tried, the more artificial her encouragement became, and she discovered a shortness of patience and a sharpness of tongue she had not known herself to possess. When she could not bear to spend one more minute trapped in a room with all those children, she simply walked out the door and left them. Guilt stopped her in the hall, and she leaned over a water fountain so passersby would see that she had only stepped out of her room for a quick break.

Laura took a deep breath and returned to her classroom. It was empty but for two desks in the front row. Waiting side by side, holding hands, sat the white-haired boy and girl.

"Who are you?" Laura demanded. "What are your names?"

"Truth," proclaimed the girl.

"Consequence," warned the boy.

Laura blinked, and they were gone.

"I've taught three times," Laura said. "Each class gets harder. I know what I want to do, but I end up doing just the opposite. And the children! Instead of learning and growing, they are developing atrocious behaviors over which I have no control. Yet Thana says I'm quickly turning into a model representative of Malison. Earning her approval is the height of success."

"And that is what you wanted." Jason nodded. "So why did you call for me?"

"I just need a sounding board, that's all." Laura softened her defensive tone and shrugged. "How can something that seems so perfectly right feel so terribly wrong?"

Jason took Laura's hands in his. "Why do you want to be a teacher, Laura?"

Her struggle with the truth produced an honest answer. "To be noticed. To finally have a voice. To be seen as someone who is smart and has value. To prove everybody wrong for doubting me and telling me I'm not good enough." She curled her fingers into fists. "But I don't want to be just any teacher at any school, and definitely not in the public sector! I want the prestige and respect of working for a private institution with an amazing reputation. And now I do." A tear crept down her cheek. "Now I do."

"Are those good reasons for wanting to teach children?" Jason asked.

"My dad was a teacher," Laura said, her voice small and sad. "I thought he would be proud of me if I followed in his footsteps."

"But his footsteps would not have led you here. I know that transparency is terrifying, Laura. It leaves you vulnerable and afraid. But the love and acceptance you need, that craving to be cherished and valued, the peace you are so desperate to find, are already yours for the asking. They are gifts designed especially for you, and they're just waiting for you to receive them. Your knight in shining armor is Jesus. Call on His name, and no power in Malison can stop you from becoming His bride and His ransomed heir."

Laura expelled a bitter sigh. "I'm not even sure I believe in God."

"You're His creation, Laura. He believes in you."

"Well, He can stop believing in me. I don't even believe in myself. I've already lied about my past, stolen materials from other instructors, and changed my students' test answers to make me and my class look better than we are. I show everyone around me the person they want to see, but inside I'm falling apart, because I know the truth about who I really am." She tried to laugh, producing a mirthless ha-ha-ha. "At least I'm keeping higher standards than most of the people here. You wouldn't believe some of the things that they do."

"It's easy to believe you're not doing as terrible a wrong as someone else when others flaunt their crimes and depravities for the world to see," Jason said gently. "But our secret sins are damaging, too – lies, vengeance, lust, anger, unforgiveness, hatred, idolatry, denial. Our private immoralities produce harmful outward results."

"You need to go." Laura's voice hardened with anger. "I don't need your righteousness ruining my life. I'm sorry I called for you. I won't bother you again."

Jason looked into Laura's eyes. "Did you know that people are praying for you, Laura? Prayer will place obstacles in your path when you're headed the wrong direction."

Laura turned her back on Jason and stalked across the room to gaze out the window into the gloom. She waited stiffly for Jason to say more, but as silence filled the room, she realized he had left her alone, as she had asked him to do.

Laura glanced at the pages Thana had placed on her desk. She blushed. "I can't present this trash to innocent children!"

"Trash?" Thana slammed her fist on the desk, and Laura cowered before the all-consuming rage of the master within. "You can, and you will," Thana said. "We must take them while they are young. Confuse them and use them, or you will lose them!"

"But they aren't old enough to be able to make their own decisions," Laura protested. "They don't have the physical or psychological maturity to apply common sense, to discern truths from deceptions. At this age, they will believe and do what any authority figure tells them to believe and do. And though I'm not their parent, it is still my responsibility to teach appropriate lessons in a manner that will help them comprehend right from wrong, so that as they grow older, they will tend toward making positive choices and decisions."

"Like you did, my dear?" Thana's grimace altered into a sarcastic smirk. "You can't teach what you don't know. You can't know what you haven't learned. You can't learn when you insist that you already know it all. Those are some of your outstanding personal qualities that we expect you to pass on to your young students–" Thana swept up the pages of sickening images and threw them in Laura's face– "while you pollute their little personalities and contaminate their little minds with anything Malison wants them to believe!"

Laura sat pale and still, her eyes closed in agonizing

submission to cravings for acceptance and approval that she could not overcome.

"Will there be anything else?" Thana demanded.

Because she needed to respond, because she wanted to know, Laura opened her eyes and looked at Thana. "Who was Edgar Bohannon?"

Thana's eyes glittered with hatred. "You've seen them. The boy and girl. They have visited you."

"Truth and Consequence," Laura dared to stay.

"Intruders!" Thana screamed. "They have interfered from the foundation of our institution. They would convince all newcomers to abandon Malison. We haven't been able to eradicate them, but we will find a way."

The question lingered. Laura looked at Thana.

"He was your predecessor, my dear. Outsiders need a deterrent to discourage their precious families from 'falling prey' to Malison, so they impose a legend on our lake."

"Edgar Lake," Laura whispered. "Oh, my God."

Thana shrieked. The master roared. Laura's world went black.

Laura roamed Malison, now a wealthy campus filled with lost souls seeking answers they would never find, now a field of ruins fallen two centuries past. It was, she discovered, a matter of perception. She, like all the other residents, portrayed a perfect life on the outside. She, like all the other residents, decayed on the inside.

She looked for Truth and Consequence as she wandered the cemetery, but she sensed that they were gone. Truth had shared her message. Consequence would bequeath the results of a choice Laura had yet to make.

She needed to talk to Jason. She called his name and saw him standing in a pool of lamplight at the corner of the nearest building, waiting for her.

"What is Malison?" she pleaded. "Who is Thana? How do I control the monster inside me that coerces me to do its will?"

"Malison is whatever you want so much that you will commit any transgression to get it. It is anything you serve in the place of our one true God."

"I don't understand," Laura said.

Jason sat on a bench and motioned for Laura to join him.

"It's a matter of worship," he said. "When you idolize an idea, you are placing your faith in a concept that is unable to hear your prayers, incapable of responding to your needs, and powerless to rescue you in times of trouble. But when God is the desire of your heart, you are in love with the one who designed you. Created you. Breathed you into being. He is able to do far more than you could ever think or ask. Trust Him with every aspect of your life, Laura, from your deepest hurts to your highest ambitions. Ask Him what He wants for you, and prepare to experience a relationship like no other."

"I want what I want," Laura insisted. "What if I trust Him, like you said, and He doesn't come through for me? What if He lets me fail again? Believe what you want, but I'm better off doing things my way."

"There is a way that seems right to each of us, but it ends in destruction." Jason looked across the campus toward the cemetery. "Sin awakens the curse, Laura. When we deliberately do wrong, we open the door to all manner of spiritual attacks from the enemy. And as you have already discovered, addiction is a demon. It accepts your invitation, and it consumes your life. You don't control it. It controls you."

"But Thana says I'm succeeding," Laura argued. "Thana says I'm becoming everything Malison should be."

Jason shook his head. "Thana is the devil's advocate. It's her job to convince you to stay until you no longer have the will to leave."

"So if I choose to stay in Malison, my life is forfeit to a curse?"

"Not merely your life," Jason said. "The devil has a contract out on your soul. If you remain in this situation, you'll continue to lose Laura, and you'll find yourself doing things you would never have dreamed of doing in your worst nightmare. Not to succeed, but to survive."

Laura hid her face with her hands, struggling with indecision. "If it just weren't so dark all the time," she complained. "Everything would be easier if there were at least one small ray of light. I'm starting to hate the night."

"Even night was created for a purpose," Jason said. "It was one of the first works of God to be defiled."

He sighed deeply as he rose to his feet. Laura stood and faced him.

"I'll call for you again," she said. "You're a true friend. I'm sorry I've been so rude."

Jason's voice softened in farewell. "You no longer need my guidance. You know the truth. You have the knowledge and the freedom to decide whether you will stay where you are or leave this illusion behind and build a genuine life for yourself."

"No, I don't!" Laura cried. "I can't leave. It hurts too much to try. I'm not strong enough to break the curse. I'm lost, and I don't know how to not be lost. You have to come back. I need you!"

"You know where your help comes from. God desires to be your salvation, your protector and closest friend. He is the light before which *no* darkness can prevail." Jason lifted Laura's hand and traced the narrow outline of a shadow that appeared as though a chain were tattooed around her wrist. "He will break every curse and set you free if you ask Him. From now on, you call on His name."

He released her hand and stepped back into the light. His smile conveyed encouragement, warmth, and love. "Your old friend Jason has to stay in Foundless. I have work to do. But I hope, and I pray, that I will look out and see you on our narrow little road returning from the lake on your way home. The world out there, the real world, needs your smile and your talents and all that God created you to be. Please, Laura, don't make the same mistake that Edgar made. Don't wait too long."

Scott stepped out of his car, taking in his surroundings as he closed the door. Faded wood and stone buildings faced each other across a half mile of two-lane road before terminating into nothing.

"And I thought ghost towns were a thing of the past," he muttered.

He mounted the creaking steps of the old country store and stepped through the open doorway, nodding at a group of locals who congregated in the corner as he walked to the cash register. The proprietor, a young man about his own age, looked up with a smile.

"Can I help you?"

"I hope so," Scott said. "I'm looking for Malison, but I've lost my way."

"Not necessarily," the proprietor said. "Maybe you've been detoured through Foundless because you're not meant to go to Malison."

"Foundless?" Scott laughed. "Is that what this one-horse town is called? Well, if you can't direct me to Malison, I'll find someone who can. I certainly didn't come here to stay."

"You came here because you're lost." An elderly man rose from a chair in the corner and ambled over to the counter. "If you're serious about pursuing Malison, you really are lost, in every way imaginable."

Scott frowned. "I don't know what you're talking about, but I'm just looking for directions. I'm not interested in a sermon."

The old man smiled. "Directions and sermons have a lot in common. Think about that while you're here. Foundless isn't a stop along your way. It's a turning point. Our little town isn't ideal for setting up housekeeping, but it's a very good place to make decisions."

"I've made my decision," Scott asserted. "I'm going to Malison."

"Then you've been offered an opportunity to reconsider. To think about what you're running from and to realize you don't know nearly enough about what you're running to. A person's perspective gets skewed when he doesn't step back from the details now and then to study the whole picture. Distance and time and thoughts and actions can become confused. Good and evil can start to look the same."

He held out his hand. "I'm Jason. This is my grandson, Lee."

"Scott," said the visitor, accepting the handshake. "I know you're trying to be helpful. But I really do need to be on my way."

A look of understanding passed between Jason and Lee. They walked to the end of the counter, and Lee motioned for Scott to follow them out the door. On the porch, Lee gestured beyond Scott's car, away from town.

"About a mile down the road, you'll see a sign pointing toward Laura Lake."

"I saw that sign," Scott said. "It looks like it's been there for a few years."

"Yes." Jason nodded sadly. "Yes, it has."

"Turn off the highway at the sign and follow the old road to the lake." As Lee provided detailed directions, a young boy appeared beside Jason holding an old metal lantern. Jason took it from him and offered it to Scott.

"It will be dark by the time you get there."

"I don't want that thing!" Scott laughed. "I have a flashlight in my car. But I would appreciate it if you'd sell me some batteries."

"Josiah will get the batteries for you. But take the lantern anyway," Jason urged. "You'll find that it will come in handy."

The boy disappeared briefly and returned with a package of batteries. He held onto it until Scott looked down at him.

"Mister Scott?"

"Yes, Josiah?"

"Beware trespassing Laura Lake."

Scott flinched at the child's solemn warning, unnerved by the intensity in the boy's eyes and the gravity of his words.

"Thank you, son," Lee said to Josiah. He smiled at Scott. "No charge."

Scott fumbled with the package for a moment and looked out into the dusk. "It is awfully late in the day," he acknowledged. "And since I don't know my way around, and I don't know anyone in Malison, maybe it would be a good idea to wait until tomorrow morning to drive out there."

Jason smiled brightly at Lee, who exhaled a sigh of relief. Lee recited directions to the town's bed and breakfast as though he had shared this conversation with many travelers many times before.

"How long you stay is up to you. While you're deciding whether you truly wish to continue on to Malison or choose a different destination, you are welcome here." Jason squeezed Scott's shoulder in farewell. "Come and see me tomorrow. I'll treat you to lunch and tell you some stories."

Scott nodded at Jason and Lee, and glanced once more at Josiah.

"Thank you," he said. "I will."

He descended the steps to his car and got in, stashing the batteries in the console. He glanced over his shoulder as he waved goodbye, startled to see the crowd, twice the number of patrons from inside the store, who waved happily in return as he pulled away and drove into town.

The Harvest Moon rises full and brilliant in the midnight sky. Mist hovers across the lake and wafts among long-neglected trees in an adjacent orchard as if bringing them to life, transforming them into ethereal, multi-limbed giants before descending to hide them from view.

A light cuts through the fog and makes its way to the farmhouse; flickers and disappears as it ventures inside; and reappears moments later in front of the barn. From there it continues to the lakeshore, where at last it becomes a lantern held aloft by a young man. A young woman clings to his arm. They pause to peer across the lake, but their destination lies obscured in darkness.

They share low conversation and quiet laughter as they make their way around the east side of the lake, searching for the bridge to their dreams. By the time they arrive, the moon has faded to a reddish haze, and the young woman murmurs a prayer that the blood on the moon might not be theirs.

He holds the lantern high. Together, they step up onto the first wooden plank.

Lights abruptly flood the grounds across Laura Lake.

Malison awaits.

More About Laura Lake:

"Malison" means "curse." The word is descended from the Latin *maledicere*, which means "to curse."

"Thana" is a Greek name meaning "death."

"Jason" is a Greek name meaning "healer."

"Lee" is a Celtic name meaning "healer."

"Josiah" is a Hebrew name meaning "Jehovah has healed."

Peacock Moon

It was a hot December night in a small Kentucky town. Most residents traitorously clicked their thermostats to the central air setting, while a contrary few basted stubbornly in their own sweat as though it were sacrilegious to resort to air conditioning so close to Christmas.

Livestock were put to worse confusion, not having the benefit of pretty girls with fancy weather maps to explain why the November blizzard that accelerated the growth of insulating fur coats abruptly fled before the advance of blazing temperatures that left them sweltering inside the shaggy mess.

The moon shone brilliant, full to overflowing. Barren trees and flat, colorless turf reflected the August-noon humidity, suffusing the landscape with a vaguely schizophrenic atmosphere.

A blood-curdling shriek shattered the suffocating tension of the night.

Annie leaped out of bed before she came fully awake. She stood still, heart pounding, skin salty-moist and panic-cold. Though instantaneously aware of the scream's origin, long moments slipped by before she regained control of her stampeding emotions.

"Help! Help! Help! *Aaaaaaagh!*"

Annie glared toward her window.

"Wretched peacocks."

The mantle clock in the living room whirred to life. Three chimes, a click, tick-tock, tick-tock. The little wooden bird in the kitchen clock concurred with a trio of "cuckoos."

Sleep chased beyond her means to catch, Annie let it go and slipped down the hall to check on her children.

They lay in twin beds against opposite walls in their spacious room. The curtains Annie had closed against the impudent moon draped wide open, and the room glowed peacefully in the lunar overflow. She walked to the window and watched her colorful trespasser wander among the shadows across her back yard. He disappeared from view without further comment, and Earth resumed her reverent silence.

Annie turned her gaze on her greatest blessings: a rambunctious ten-year-old, oblivious to danger or fear, and an eight-year-old wise beyond such pitifully few years. Her daughters. Plainly beautiful, country fresh, honeysuckle sweet, wild as the tornadic winds that swept them into the world. Two years apart to the day, to the minute. Annie wondered how often such miracles occurred.

April spread-eagled across her bed in naked abandon, ever reckless asleep as when awake, and she slept as hard as she played.

Amanda's eyes were open, studying her mother in the moonlight. Annie padded to her youngest daughter's side and kissed the child between those wide, amazingly blue eyes.

"Did the peacock scare you, Mom?"

"Until I realized what it was," Annie admitted. "Did it scare you?"

"No." Amanda sighed. "I was awake anyway."

"Want some milk, or a glass of water?"

"No. I just want to lie here. I want to watch the moon."

"It's so bright. It'll keep you awake," Annie protested.

"I pretend it's Daddy," Amanda whispered, "and he's looking back at me. I talk to him sometimes."

Her words drifted away before Annie could catch them, hold them, respond to their need. One tear made the short trek across

Amanda's small nose, and Annie kissed it away.

"He loves you, baby. And so do I."

"I love you, too, Mom."

Annie crept to April's side with unnecessary caution and kissed the back of her neck where long, sandy hair swept high across the pillow. April breathed deeply and did not stir.

Annie paused at the door. Day or night, she could not enter her daughters' room without feeling she had crossed a threshold onto sacred ground. That their sanctuary resulted from conflict added humor to holiness.

When they moved into the house two years ago, the girls chose to share a room. Arguments promptly ensued as to how it would be painted.

"I want my room to look like summertime!" April twirled with excitement.

"I want my walls to be plain white!" Amanda stated flatly. Arms crossed. Determined.

Annie ended the argument by telling the girls they could each have their own room.

"No!" The sisters immediately clasped hands and faced her as though *she* were the problem. "We want our room to be together, please, Mom!"

Anticipation in April's shining eyes. Stubborn tears in Amanda's.

It was all Annie could do to keep from rolling hers.

"If, and only if, the two of you can agree on colors and décor," she told them. "By tonight," she added. "The rest of our furniture arrives next week, and I want our house ready by the time it gets here."

That evening her little girls brought her a detailed shopping list. The next day she took them to Home Depot and pushed a cart behind them for three hours as they discussed their plans with each other, even asking a clerk for assistance, while she smiled quietly and enjoyed their enthusiasm at being trusted to make such a monumental decision for themselves.

They vetoed her request to "Let me see what you've picked

out," even unloading the cart in the check-out line by themselves. Annie swallowed down her reaction at the expense and swiped her debit card without comment. They had been through so much, her precious girls, and had reacted with far more strength than she found in herself. They deserved to have some fun.

April and Amanda directed the painting of the pale sky overhead and the walls – winter snow on one side, spring green on the other – while they arranged strings of clear lights on swaths of gauzy white fabric. Attached to the ceiling, draped to meet above the center of each bed, the canopies lent warmth and peace to the night.

"Fireflies!" April cheered, and Annie set her lights to blink slowly in alternating patterns.

"Stars," Amanda insisted. Her lights stayed on solid.

Annie set up a platform so April could reach the sky and stood guard while April painted the sun and the moon as she knew them – gentle, ancient faces, one extending luxurious, wavy rays, the other spangled with stardust – using glow-in-the-dark paints.

Amanda protested. "The sun doesn't shine at night!"

"The sun never goes out," April told her. "Even at night when the world is dark, the sun is still shining. All you have to do is wait and see."

Annie stayed busy for the rest of the week, painting rooms and hanging wallpaper with family and friends. On the morning the furniture was to be delivered, April and Amanda invited their mother through their door to view their handiwork. Annie felt as though she had entered a cathedral. The girls had transformed their room, leaving only the polished oak floor unchanged.

A meadow of wildflowers bloomed along April's walls, not a cluttered riot of color, but individual blossoms atop long slender stems rising from so many nuances of green – deep shadows here, where a spray of wild roses arched above a stone, almost golden there, where sunlight filtered through blades of grass – that nature herself would have applauded the child's passion. Butterflies and hummingbirds tended April's garden. An alert frog sat on a lily pad, poised to leap into the corner pond. A peacock stood tall beside April's bed, his fanned tail partially obscured by the purple irises among which he lingered.

At the straight line down the facing walls where her half of the room met Amanda's, flower petals and dandelion seed tufts wafted upward off April's flowers across the first two feet of Amanda's white walls, as though carried aloft on a breeze. Beyond that invasion of color, Amanda's side of the room remained emotionless and empty. No prints on her walls, no knickknacks on shelves or toys atop the trunk at the foot of her bed. She adamantly kept her life devoid of personal touches but for the stuffed pony with a clear photo pocket on each side of his saddle. Photos of Amanda's father occupied those pockets, and Amanda slept with the pony every night.

Annie sent up a prayer for her girls as she stepped out of their room. She flinched as soft, plush fur smoothed past her ankles. A pair of ginger tabbies trotted into the room on velvet paws and leaped onto Amanda's bed with silent grace, landing whisper-soft on her pillow. The stout male proceeded across the headboard to the windowsill, where he assumed guardianship of his territory. The slender female curled into the curve of Amanda's body, fitting her head under the girl's chin, purring and kneading as Amanda snuggled around her.

"Good kids," Annie murmured to the cats. She left the door open so the feline siblings could come and go as they pleased.

She wandered through the house, rechecking doors and windows. She paused to caress the wedding photo on the mantle: she and her beloved husband, smiling a dozen years innocent of the framed Purple Heart and the reverently-folded American flag that watched over the memory of that happy couple.

The peacock shrilled out another series of raucous cries. What a contradiction that one of the world's most exquisite creatures should possess the most haunting, unnerving voice. Annie's imagination formed the frantic plea in their call. She found it ironic that peafowl could broadcast the word, loud and pointless, while she intensely longed for help, but couldn't bring herself to ask for it.

How ridiculous to envy a bird.

"I miss you," she breathed, caressing the photo. "God, how I miss you."

No man could have been more loving and dedicated. Four idyllic years produced two beautiful children, but lay-offs and a lack of employment opportunities led Drew to pursue his childhood dream of becoming a soldier. He joined the United States Army, proud of the opportunity to provide for his family by serving his country. Separation was excruciating, but he and Annie loved each other and wrote to each other and prayed for each other, counting days and hours, knowing deployment was a temporary condition of his commitment to Uncle Sam, that before they both knew it, they would be celebrating his homecoming in each other's arms.

And they did, at the conclusion of every deployment, through years of promotions and transfers to bases across the country. They celebrated until one final deployment took Drew to a war zone. He returned home three months later in a casket draped with an American flag, welcomed upon arrival by soldiers and patriots and friends, escorted to his final resting place by his entire hometown, and ushered into eternity with full military honors.

The two and a half years since were sometimes a lifetime, often only a moment ago. April had been eight years old, Amanda only six when Annie had to explain that Daddy got assigned a permanent change of station to Heaven and this transfer was forever, which meant they wouldn't be able to see him again until God was ready for them to join him there.

At Drew's funeral, everyone mourned but April. At the 21-gun salute, she cheered and danced. "That's my Dad! I love you, Dad!" She did not comprehend the finality of death. To her, Dad wasn't a corpse in a grave. He was very much alive in Heaven, as eager as she was for a family reunion. Far from grieving, she was awed that he actually got to meet Jesus in person and see Him every day, and she happily anticipated joining them.

Amanda lingered at the opposite end of the spectrum. The day of Drew's funeral eased into a night vibrant with a brilliant full moon, and Amanda had worshipped the moon ever after. She didn't grasp the concept of Heaven, but she understood clearly the grave into which her father's casket disappeared. For the first several weeks, Amanda begged daily to be taken to Drew's gravesite so she could "talk to Daddy." Gradually she came to realize that her hero really was gone, that death was irreversible, and that her prayers were not going to bring him home ever again. And the child reacted with hurt and resentment toward the God who killed her daddy.

Annie unlocked the front door and stepped out into the stifling humidity. She walked to the corner of the porch and leaned against the railing for only a moment before covert noises from the rear of the house caught her attention.

April, now in her nightgown, emerged from the shadows and trotted across the back lawn toward the barn.

"What on earth," Annie sighed, hurrying after the girl.

April stood just outside the shadow of the barn holding an empty scoop. A pair of peafowl pecked up the grains of dry cat food she had scattered across the packed dirt lane.

"April!"

"Hi, Mom! Why are you up?"

"A better question, young lady, is why you are feeding cat food to peacocks in the wee hours of the morning."

"Raja was hungry." April nodded toward the male, who tilted his head and studied her sideways. April laughed and held out her hand. The huge bird carefully gobbled up the kibble she offered.

"He could have waited for breakfast, like the rest of us," Annie said.

"He wasn't just asking for himself," April said. "Rani wanted cat food, and he told her he'd get her some."

"And just how do you know what that peacock is thinking?"

"He told me." April looked at Annie as though a perplexed that she didn't grasp the obvious. "I told him I would give them a whole scoop if they would be quiet so we can sleep through the rest of the night."

"What did he say to that?" Annie smiled.

"Well, they're quiet now, aren't they?" April stroked the peacock's back, and he stood perfectly still, as though demonstrating to his hen that this human was his friend.

April reached for Annie's hand. "Let's go back to bed, Mom. They won't make any more noise tonight."

Annie allowed her daughter to lead her back into the kitchen. April drank a glass of water and returned to bed.

Annie walked through the house and locked the front door. She took the wedding photo from the mantle and hugged it close as she curled up on the sofa, where she fell asleep with Drew in her arms.

"Wake up, Mom! It's Monday! We have to get ready for our home school classes at the church!" April charged into the living room and stopped short at the sight of her mother sleeping on the sofa, Amanda in her arms, both wadded under a blanket topped with two round cushions of purring orange fur.

April lifted her parents' wedding picture from the pile and, using the hem of her shirt, gently wiped her mother's fingerprints from her father's face. She carried the photograph to the fireplace, stepped up onto the hearth, and carefully returned the memory to the mantle.

Annie stirred, waking Amanda. The cats stretched and yawned widely.

"I'll feed Samson and Soleil," April said. The cats leaped to the floor and trotted ahead of her toward the kitchen.

"Don't forget their litterboxes," Annie called after her.

"Already done," April said.

By the time Annie and Amanda had completed their morning routines, April had breakfast waiting in the nook off the kitchen.

Annie sipped her coffee gratefully as she sat down to scrambled eggs, sausage, and toast. She looked into her daughter's smiling face and pushed aside her guilt at sleeping late. She took another look at the place settings and frowned.

April answered before she could ask. "Bryan is joining us."

"You invited him?" Annie asked indignantly.

"No." April poured juice in four glasses.

"Oh. He invited himself." Annie scowled into her coffee.

"No." April wiped her hands on a towel.

"Then who did?" Annie demanded.

"No one. He's dropping by on his way home from work, so I fixed enough breakfast for all of us."

"Okay." Annie sat down her mug and faced her daughter. "You're saying no one invited him. Did he call while I was in the shower? How do you know he's on his way?"

Annie was treated to another of April's patient, enigmatic looks. "I just do." She shrugged and headed toward the hall.

"Where are you going?" Annie called after her.

"To let him in, Mom."

Annie hurried to the kitchen window. A full five seconds ticked by before Bryan's truck came into view at the gap in the trees down their gravel lane, a half mile away. She sighed deeply and returned to her seat in the breakfast nook.

"Miss Simon says she has a problem with April." Though Principal Dennis spoke politely, Annie heard "again" in his voice.

Simon says. April's second-grade year. They lived in California then. When school started, Annie had to resist the urge to laugh every time April prefaced a comment with, "Miss Simon says!" Daily accusations against April resulted in a three-month-long list of misdeeds for which April endured punishment from Miss Simon and derision from her fellow students.

The teacher wanted April out of her class. She told Annie this in no uncertain terms in the presence of Principal Dennis. April didn't behave like other seven-year-olds. She conversed with adults as though she were their equal, aced every assignment with no apparent effort, and talked aloud with her peers about thoughts and actions they committed only in the privacy of their own minds.

The other children responded by mocking April and calling her names. Miss Simon not only permitted their abuse, but encouraged it by laughing with them at the strange child who tilted her head and looked into their minds, saw the fear and confusion there, and chose not to retaliate in word or deed.

They went too far the day an older girl tripped April and slammed her face against the pavement as the children played tag in the parking lot at recess. April's classmates gathered around and laughed as blood poured from her nose and from the gash on her chin. April looked up at the circle of leering faces, uncomprehending.

"Why are you laughing at me? I'm hurt! I need help!" April struggled to a kneeling position in a pool of her own blood. They laughed all the harder.

"Why do you think it's funny that I'm hurt?" April asked. "Do you not understand what it means to be injured, or are you just cruel?"

The laughter stopped. The children looked at each other uncertainly until one boy answered her question by spitting into her hair and calling her a vulgar name.

Before April had a chance to respond, Miss Simon intervened, elbowing her way through the crowd to discover the source of the playground's amusement. She took April to the school nurse's office to hold a compress to her face and to call Annie.

On the way to the emergency room, April demanded an explanation.

"Why, Mom? Why did she deliberately hurt me? Did all those kids honestly think it was funny that I was injured and bleeding? And that boy, Dugan! Why did he curse at me and spit on me when I asked a simple question?"

Annie struggled to restrain her fury against Miss Simon for fostering the hostile environment that led to the attack against April, for not calling an ambulance, for actually suggesting the incident might have been April's fault. Annie offered the only excuse that came to mind. "They are ignorant, ill-mannered kids. They have lot of learning to do."

"Well, they're learning the wrong things!" April retorted. "They need better teachers! They aren't ignorant, either. They knew exactly what they were doing, and they did it on purpose!" She leaned back against the seat and closed her eyes. "I saw darkness in their minds, Mom. And something blacker than darkness. It doesn't like me. I was scared."

"April, honey." Annie gripped the steering wheel and shared a brutal truth with her innocent girl. "There is no explanation for evil, April. It just *is*."

Five stitches ensured the gash on April's chin would heal to a tiny, barely noticeable white line. The stitches came out long before the bruises faded from across her nose and forehead. The questions remained. April wasn't angry. She didn't have it in her to hold a grudge. But she had hit upon a curiosity. She wanted, needed to know why her classmates had reacted to her injuries with savage ridicule instead of with compassion and assistance.

The school paid April's medical bills. Principal Dennis relieved Miss Simon of her responsibilities and encouraged her to seek employment outside the school district. A social services agent enrolled the girl who attacked April in an anger management program and scheduled weekly visits with the girl's mother in their home.

April left the emergency room physician no choice but to answer her detailed questions about her injuries and the healing process. Not knowing how to react to the child's intelligence and insight, he insisted to Annie that April needed to take prescription drugs commonly administered to hyperactive children.

"She isn't hyperactive. On the contrary, April is very mature for her age," Annie argued.

"Which is obviously a problem. One chewable tablet every day should take the edge off her adventurous nature." He sent them home with a bottle of pills and orders to follow up with their family doctor.

When April received a reprimand from her new teacher on her first day back to school for pointing out a series of mistakes in a textbook, Annie took another look at the pills. Lord knows, she had tried everything she could think of to help her daughter behave like a normal little girl.

Annie gave April one dose before dinner, and the child awoke in the night sobbing, "It's got me, Mom! Make it stop!"

Terrified, Annie pulled April onto her lap and held her tight. "Nothing's got you, honey. Mama's right here."

"In here, it's in here!" April wailed, pointing to her head and her heart. "It's got me, it's holding me down, I can think, or be, or breathe!"

April hugged herself, rocking back and forth in Annie's lap. She squeezed her eyes closed and screamed from the depths of her soul.

"Mommy! I can't find myself, Mommy! Birds are just birds and clouds are just clouds and God is just a man and stories are just words! Colors won't sing and music won't dance and animals won't talk to me! The part of me that they knew isn't me anymore! It's dark inside! I'm drowning! Help me, Mommy, help me, *help me!*"

Not since April's infancy had Annie seen her daughter cry. She held April until the drug wore off, and she grieved for the weeks that passed before her daughter's spirit recovered from her encounter with that ominous, man-made oppression.

Annie made the decision to home school her children. She dropped the bottle of pills into the prescription drug bin at the nearest police department. She and April never discussed the incident again, and Annie never told Drew about the troubles they endured while he was away.

"Good morning!" Bryan's smile lit up the room as he lowered April to the floor, accepted a half-hearted hug from Amanda, and dropped into a chair across from Annie. "Thanks for breakfast. I'm starved."

One glimpse of the warmth in Bryan's sparkling eyes was enough to spiral Annie into a vortex of desire, relief, and determined resistance. She focused on her toast. "It was April's idea."

"April, everything looks delicious. Thank you for cooking for us."

"I like to do it." April sat next to Bryan and placed her hand in his. "Will you pray a blessing upon our day?"

Bryan squeezed her hand and reached across the table to clasp Annie's. Amanda joined hands with her mother and her sister, and the circle was complete.

Annie bowed her head, acutely aware of Bryan's hand engulfing hers, of strength courageous enough to battle a raging fire or rescue a victim from twisted wreckage, yet gentle enough to pray with a child.

Yet it was all she could do to keep from jerking her hand away before he concluded the prayer.

"Amen!" the girls said in unison.

"How are your tree cats?" April offered Brian a slice of toast.

"I haven't seen them for a couple of days. But Gina would let me know if they were anything less than their usual perfect selves."

"Tree cats," Amanda scoffed.

"They were all rescued from trees," April pointed out.

"Who is Gina?" Annie was furious at herself for having asked the question aloud, but if Bryan noticed her embarrassment, he had the grace to not let her know.

"My neighbor's daughter," he said. "She takes care of the cats before and after school while I am at work."

"Where does she go to school?" Amanda wanted to know, and Bryan told the girls all about the latest adventures of his three felines, about the teenager who took care of them during his 48-hour shifts at the fire department, and his plans for his days off.

"Did you watch the morning news?" he asked.

"We overslept," Amanda said.

"The weather is becoming a concern." Bryan looked at Annie. "Low-lying areas are still flooded from the heavy thaw and torrential rains of last month's winter storm. Creeks are out of their banks, and the river continues to rise as it receives runoff from higher altitudes. The storm prediction center is forecasting a potential for severe thunderstorms with possible tornados and several inches of rain starting this weekend. A lot of our community is going to be under water if that happens."

"But it's December!" Amanda protested. "Christmas is less than three weeks away. We're going to start decorating this weekend. What happened to winter?"

"We should build levees," April said.

"Winter is in a strange mood this year," Bryan agreed. "National Guard troops are arriving as we speak. Emergency services, churches, and volunteer groups are already building those levees and preparing to open shelters for those who have to evacuate their homes." He caught Annie's gaze. "With your permission, I'd like to take a look at Apple Creek where it cuts through your farm. If we build a levee on this side of the creek to protect the subdivisions to the southwest, it will have to extend across your property. That puts your house on the safe side as well."

Annie nodded. "Whatever you need to do is fine. What can I do to help?"

"I'll help fill sandbags," April said.

"Only after school," Bryan said.

"It's okay. I graduate from high school on Friday. I start college after Christmas break," April said, as though it were perfectly normal for a ten-year-old to enroll in college.

Bryan exhibited no surprise. "Have you chosen a major?"

April shook her head and expelled a deep sigh. "It's hard to choose just one or two. I want to learn them all!"

"And why can't you?" Bryan smiled. "Not all at once, of course, but no one says you can't keep earning college degrees for as long as you wish."

April graced her mother with her third enigmatic gaze in less than six hours. "Or for as long as I live," she said to Bryan.

"She's been called a savant," Annie told Bryan as they walked to the creek. "But her knowledge is inherent, not learned. Gifted, but her abilities are inborn, not the result of training or practice. Clairvoyant, because sometimes she knows things she couldn't possibly know. Telepathic, because she communicates with animals, with the elements, with God on a level I can't begin to understand. But not with people. She says people are unwilling to communicate that way because they have too much to hide."

Bryan opened the gate to the west pasture and followed Annie through.

"One doctor suggested autism because he couldn't think of any other label to apply to a child no one understands." Annie brushed away a tear. "Not even me. But he admitted that with April, nothing is lacking. On the contrary, too much is there. And while everyone else, including me, struggles with our perceptions of her, April is perfectly comfortable with, and confident in, herself. She is the only one who knows what she is about."

"Pastor Sherman called her an angel."

Annie turned to Bryan, surprised. "When was this?"

"The first Sunday you brought your family to church, right after you moved here. April walked up to me after service, called my name, and took me by the hand as if she'd known me forever. I asked the pastor if he knew this smart, beautiful little girl, and he said he had just met her himself. He said it was the first time in his life an angel ever walked up to him, took him by the hand, and called him by name. Funny thing is, I think he was serious!"

"April knows things other people don't know and can't learn." Annie dug a tissue from her pocket and dried her eyes. "How do you explain that to people?"

"I don't suppose you can," Bryan said. He reached for her hand.

"There appears to be nothing that April can't do. Her artistic and musical talents rival the most elite professionals. Her communion with nature and her ability to read people are beyond understanding. Her automatic knowledge of any topic from science to theology puts experts to shame. Adults are awed by her. They call her a miracle. But her peers, other kids her age, are malicious. They've called her a freak, a witch, names I love God too much to repeat. When verbal abuse escalated to a physical attack three years ago, I took her out of public school and began teaching her and Amanda at home. The mundane expectations of ordinary education insulted her intelligence anyway. Like wrapping chains around her wings. You know?"

"I know."

"Her education is about to exceed mine. I'm not going to enroll a ten-year-old in a university. I have friends who are college instructors. They've promised to teach her whatever she wishes to learn until she is at least fifteen. Perhaps then we can apply for scholarships and enroll her in the community college. She might be allowed to take online classes for credit in the meantime."

"Forgive me if I'm speaking out of turn," Bryan said, "but I have no doubt that April would excel at college level work. I think she's ready for it."

Annie produced a wry smile. "I agree. April is ready for college. Trouble is, college isn't ready for April."

The roar of rushing water drowned out further conversation. Annie's eyes widened as she and Bryan stopped on the hill above Apple Creek. The once-peaceful stream stampeded violently across the field, muddy and littered with branches.

"The horses." She turned to Bryan, shouting to be heard. "Mr. Jackson leases this field and the barn for his horses."

"If we build a levee across the slope right where we're standing, they should be all right," Bryan said.

"I'll call him," Annie said. "If the storms do come, he may want to move them until the worst is over."

"What about April's peafowl?" Bryan asked as they retreated from the creek and walked back across the pasture.

Annie shook her head. "They belong to Mr. English. His farm backs up to mine. He lives a mile away, but his birds roam free. Those two arrived in my back yard last spring. When I tried to chase them away, they flew to the roof of my garden shed and perched there, observing their realm from above elevated beaks."

Annie laughed with Bryan. "They bonded with April as if they'd always known her. They communicate with her. She says peacocks usually have a harem, but Raja is committed solely to Rani. They are always together. April says they love each other." Annie shrugged. "I guess it's possible. When they first showed up, I spoke to Mr. English about coming to get them."

"But he gave them to April," Bryan said.

"He did. He told me he would continue to take care of any medical needs they might have. He built a pen behind our barn so we can confine them and bring them into the barn during inclement weather. He showed April how to create a nesting box, though Rani hasn't produced eggs yet. I guess you could say they're his by right, hers by heart."

Annie looked up into Bryan's face, grateful for his understanding smile. Their eyes met and held, and Annie reacted to the threat of intimacy by turning her gaze to the ground. This was the longest and most intimate conversation she had shared with Bryan, and she was shocked at how easily and completely she had opened up to him. She retreated from his touch and pulled her emotional barriers firmly back into place before her mind could lose its control over her heart.

They talked politely the rest of the way back to the house. Bryan respected Annie's aloofness. Unlike countless times before, this morning he didn't take her hand or smile into her eyes or ask her to bring the girls by his house to visit his cats or invite her to join him for coffee or for dinner.

When they reached the driveway, Bryan accepted April's offer to help her feed Raja and Rani. After the birds had eaten, he hugged April and Amanda goodbye and reminded Annie to call him if she needed anything.

Then he drove away, leaving Annie bewildered and angry at herself for wishing he had at least attempted to challenge the line she had tacitly forbidden him to cross.

Amanda sat on the living room floor in her pajamas, a photo album open on her lap. She frowned at the pictures with deep concern, waiting for someone to notice. When Annie and April remained oblivious to her displeasure, she gave it a voice.

"Bryan likes you." She stared hard at her mother. "You should tell him to stay away from us."

"Bryan loves you." The smile April directed at Annie faded when she turned to her sister. "Bryan is genuine. He is a wonderful person. He loves you and me, too, and Samson and Soleil, and even Raja and Rani. Why are you angry?"

"You're never sad like Mom and me!" Amanda accused. "You don't cry for Daddy. You don't even care that he's gone!"

April looked at Amanda as though the younger girl had lost her mind. "Dad's in Heaven! He's happier than any of us can imagine. Why would I cry for him?"

"You would cry if you missed him!" Amanda shot back. "Mom does, and I do!"

"You are crying for yourself," April said, "because you are lonely without him. Of course I miss Dad, but my grief is for our loss, not for the perfection that Dad has gained. Cry for yourself all you want, but there's no reason to cry for Dad."

Amanda knew better than to stomp out of the room. Her mother had taught her better manners than that. Her face reddened with anger at the truth her sister had shared. She climbed into the recliner and sat with her back to Annie and April, staring at photos blurred by the tears in her eyes and the aching void in her heart.

Annie sat stunned at April's revelation, stinging at the unintended reprimand.

"Dad couldn't stand to see you sad." April spoke softly to her mother. "When you used to cry, he would hold you close and tell jokes to make you laugh. He would show you that there was more to life than whatever you were upset about. If he was here with us right now, he'd do everything in his power to make sure we were all happy. Dad would be really upset if he thought we were feeling sorry for ourselves instead of taking care of each other like we always did when the army took him away from us for long periods of time."

Annie didn't know what to say. She held out her arms to both of her girls. April came to her at once and took refuge in her mother's embrace. Amanda concentrated on her anger until her tears spilled over, and she joined her family on the sofa and sobbed in her mother's arms.

An hour later Annie lay in bed staring at the ceiling, reliving the day. April's parting words hovered like a shroud of encouragement and denial, joy and fear.

"Daddy wouldn't sentence you to solitude just because God called him to Heaven first. He knows you have more love to give than Amanda and I could ever use up. Don't be afraid of hurting Daddy's feelings. Don't be afraid of letting Bryan love you. And don't be afraid to open your heart."

In the privacy of her own mind, Annie acknowledged that April was right. She admitted that she was lonely, sometimes excruciatingly so, but her heart belonged to her husband, and she would never, could never, be unfaithful to Drew. She reluctantly conceded to finding Bryan dangerously attractive, emotionally and spiritually as well as physically. His attention told her she was wanted, and his concern told her that he cared deeply for her and her daughters. But Annie reminded herself that she didn't want a future relationship with any man, especially one with a dangerous career that could leave her widowed once more.

When all the mental arguments and emotional battles were put to rest, one fact remained. The truest reason Annie remained single and dateless lay awake in the next room gazing at the moonlight under feline guard, grieving her dreams away one teardrop at a time.

"April!" Drew's frantic voice brought Annie to the front yard at a dead run. "April, be still. Daddy's coming to get you. Just don't move!"

Four-year-old April walked the ridgepole of the roof like a

gymnast on a balance beam. Spread her arms wide, performed three cartwheels, a backbend, a handstand complete with splits. She applauded herself and took a bow.

"It's okay, Daddy! God's got me!"

By the time Drew pulled the ladder from the garage, April had climbed down the tree whose branches spread over the roof. She dropped the last five feet and rolled like an acrobat right into her father's arms.

Annie woke from the dream to the sound of her daughter's exuberant laughter, soothing and confident and certain to her soul.

"Hi, Annie." Bryan's smile melted her heart in an instant.

Enough that there were so many real dangers. She was weary of defending herself from imaginary threats. She smiled and pushed open the screened door.

"Hey, Bryan. Come on in."

She led him through the living room and into the kitchen. "Would you like a glass of tea?"

"Thanks."

She saw caution in his smile. Had he become so accustomed to her constant rejection that he didn't trust her welcome to be genuine? Annie felt ashamed.

"The girls and I baked a blueberry pie last night." She cut a slice and placed it on a saucer. "We picked the blueberries ourselves back in the summer. We have a freezer full of them. I'll give you several bags to take home if you like." She added a scoop of ice cream and offered him his usual chair in the breakfast nook.

Bryan took a bite of the pie as Annie sat down to face him. "This," he proclaimed, "is outstanding." He took another bite and looked around. "Where are April and Amanda?"

"They're in school. Homeschooling is a community effort. I'm good with English and history, so I teach those subjects to homeschooled students in a classroom at our church twice a week. Other parents teach other subjects at different times, and we all teach our children various lessons at home every day. Today Amanda is in a geography class, and April is meeting with a biology professor from the community college."

"You're an amazing woman, Annie. Please – " Bryan held up his hands. "Please don't be angry with me for saying that. I'm not making a pass at you, I'm not intruding into your life, I'm not using friendship with your daughters as a route to a relationship with you. I'm just offering you a compliment."

The tears came instantly. Annie bowed her head and closed her eyes, hoping he wouldn't see, wouldn't discover how very wounded she was.

"I understand," Bryan continued quietly. "You've tolerated my friendship, and I appreciate that. I do care about you, Annie. I won't lie. There's nothing I wouldn't do for you and those beautiful girls."

He laid his fork across the half-eaten pie and pushed the saucer away.

"I almost forgot why I stopped by." He slid a small box across the table. "It's a battery-operated weather radio. I know you have a weather app on your phone, but if you're not carrying it, you won't be aware of a watch or a warning, and if the cell towers are damaged or destroyed, the phone will be useless anyway. The forecast isn't good, Annie. That's why I want you to have this, so the storms won't catch you off guard."

Bryan stood. "Thank you for the pie. It's delicious. Tell the girls 'hello' for me."

He was through the kitchen doorway before Annie realized he was leaving.

Everything in her screamed for her to go after him, but she sat still and released the tears that needed to fall. She heard the front door latch gently behind him as she sobbed into a linen Christmas napkin that Amanda had picked out the year before, because she liked the golden stars sprinkled across the burgundy background.

April and Amanda. Her sun and her stars.

"Help! Help! Help!" Raja shouted.

"*Aaaaaaagh!*" cried Rani.

Annie bolted for the door, calling Bryan's name as she ran out onto the porch, arriving just in time to see the taillights of his truck disappear around the bend out of sight.

"How can you not be mad at God for taking Daddy away from us?"

Annie overheard Amanda pose the question to April as the girls unpacked a box of Christmas decorations in the living room floor. Though she usually avoided eavesdropping on her daughters, Annie stopped loading the dishwasher in order to hear their conversation.

"Because God didn't," April said. "Dad was killed by an IED placed in the path of his truck by our enemy. He wasn't the only one. Three other soldiers died in that attack."

"But why?" Amanda started to cry. "Why do they hate us and other people so much that they want to kill us all? And why does God let it happen?"

"People do things to each other that God never intended," April replied softly. "Mom told me once that there is no explanation for evil. It just *is*. And the only real way we can oppose it is by holding fast to our faith in God and to our love for each other. Even when it seems impossible, because we're angry and sad; even when we need to attack something in retaliation, but there's nothing or no one to get even with. When we don't think we're able to love anyone else, we need to let ourselves be loved. It won't be long before we receive enough love that we can start loving God and other people and ourselves again."

"But how can I go on without Daddy?" Amanda wailed, and Annie heard April push the box aside in order to wrap her arms around her sister.

"You don't," April assured her. "You don't, because you are part of Dad, and he's part of you. His blood will always run through your veins, and his love will always fill your heart. You don't get over his death. You just gradually come to realize that death isn't an end; it's a threshold; and it's going to be a long time before you see Dad again, but you *will* see him again."

"I'm sorry for what I said the other night," Amanda said. "I know you miss him, too. You just don't show it like Mom and I do."

"I write letters to Dad and read them to God," April said, "and God makes sure Dad hears my heart."

Annie heard the girls crying together and started to go to them, until Amanda spoke again.

"Will you pray with me, April? I don't want to be angry anymore. I want to be close to God like you are. I want to see things brighter and happier like you do. And I don't want to hurt anybody else's feelings anymore just because I've been hurt."

Annie stood out of sight beyond the kitchen doorway and wept quietly as she silently joined her daughters in prayer.

"They aren't going to get the levee built in time," April announced Thursday morning. "It's already starting to rain. Rani is nervous. I'm going to bring her and Raja into the barn."

"Put on your raincoat, and be careful." Annie stared out the window.

"He isn't coming," April said.

Annie didn't move.

"His shift started this morning. He'll be at work until Saturday." April slipped into her raincoat. "Mom, you don't know anything about Bryan. He's talked with you a lot about us. He's taken the time to learn about you. But you haven't asked him a single question about his past or his family or his outlook on life."

"I didn't want to encourage him," Annie said, as though speaking with an equal. "I didn't want him to love me when I can't love him back. It wouldn't be fair to him."

April stood still and waited.

"I'm not going to turn around and look at you," Annie informed her.

"You don't have to look at me to see the truth," April said gently. "The truth is in your heart, and it refuses to be hidden anymore. Mom, it's okay to be broken, because you *are*. It's okay to be uncertain, because you *are*. God loves you broken and uncertain, so it's okay to love yourself that way, too."

Annie wiped away a tear.

"And it's okay to be afraid, but you don't have to be afraid of Bryan, because he has experienced death and loss and fear and anger. He knows all about starting over and putting your life back together. He knows how it hurts to have to learn to live alone when, for years, you've been half of a whole."

Annie sat down and took April's hands in hers. "What do you mean?"

April smiled. "You'll have to ask Bryan."

"But you said he's not coming back."

"If he doesn't, you can always go to him. Just don't wait too long, okay?" April kissed her mother on the cheek and trotted out the kitchen door into the rain.

Storm sirens and a vicious crack of lightning woke Annie early Friday morning. Rain began as a deluge that pounded the earth and whipped horizontal in gale force winds.

The weather radio broadcast constant alerts. At midday the storm knocked out the electricity. Annie collected flashlights and candles, water bottles and snacks, and herded the girls and the cats to the basement, where they spent the afternoon listening to storm warnings and playing board games. When Annie suggested they sleep fully clothed and pretend they were camping out, April and Amanda went along with the façade. They curled up on the futon and told each other ghost stories by flashlight until Annie announced bedtime. She prayed with her children, and they lay down and tried to sleep.

Silence woke Annie Saturday morning, unnerving after twenty-four hours of roaring torrential rains and the nonstop blare of storm warnings. She shifted under the blanket, waking Amanda. They were alone. April must have gone upstairs, probably to feed the cats and start breakfast.

Annie sat up and swung her bare feet the floor, alarmed to find herself ankle deep in icy water.

"Sit still until I turn on a flashlight," she told Amanda.

In the few minutes it took to collect the items she and the girls had brought down the day before, the water had risen another inch. Annie carried Amanda to the steps and sent her upstairs with half the load. She glanced around. The futon would be soaked. The end tables would probably survive. The washer and dryer probably wouldn't, but she couldn't do anything about that. The few boxes of stored items sat up on shelves, and the basement was a walk-out. The water couldn't rise into the house upstairs.

"Mom." Amanda's voice called Annie to the kitchen window as she closed the door at the top of the basement steps.

Annie approached the window in the semi-darkness, shivering in the unaccustomed cool of the morning. Her heart sank at the view across their back yard.

Rain continued to fall in a steady downpour, still whipped by brutal gusts of wind. Their house was an island in the midst of a shallow lake. Half the barn lay in splinters under an uprooted tree. The back porch awning dammed an overflowing ditch, and Annie's garden shed was completely gone, leaving only a concrete pad to indicate it had existed at all.

"The barn is destroyed," Amanda breathed. "Oh, Mom, Raja and Rani were in there!"

Annie's blood ran cold. "Where is April?"

"She fed Samson and Soleil." Amanda absently studied the two cats grooming on the kitchen rug. "But I haven't seen her since I came upstairs."

"April!" Annie ran to the girls' room and found it empty. She returned to the kitchen and threw open the door and went still at the path of frost-rimmed, water-filled pocks in the mud disappearing toward the barn.

"The hot weather blew away with the storms," Amanda observed. "It's winter again. Sleet is mixed with the rain." She grasped Annie's arm and pointed at the row of hooks above the bench beside the door. "April's heavy coat and boots are gone."

"Call 9-1-1!" Annie sat on the bench and pulled on her boots.

"The phones are dead!"

Annie tossed her mobile phone to Amanda and grabbed her raincoat.

"No cell service, either. I'll go for help, Mom. I'll cut through the field to Mr. Jackson's place."

"No!" Annie yelled. "You stay right here, *right here!* I'll go find April."

Annie rushed out the door and tried to run. She fell to her knees as her boots caught in the suction of mud and standing water. She clambered to her feet and slogged across the back yard to the lane leading to the barn.

"April!" she shouted. It occurred to Annie from a distance that silence deafens the chaos of a storm when you're listening for one specific voice that doesn't answer. She called out to April again, and even to Raja and Rani, but only the freezing rain and keening wind uttered a response.

The front of the barn leaned precariously against the enormous fallen tree. Annie realized immediately that there was no back half to enter, no way to sort through the broken boards and sheets of metal roofing that lay strewn under the massive branches. She tried anyway, crying out for her daughter, searching for any evidence of long sandy hair or iridescent feathers, for she knew that where she found the peafowl, she would find April.

The call carried from the field straight through her heart.

"Help! Help! *Help!*"

"Raja," Annie whispered.

She shook so hard from the cold that her whole body ached. The temperature continued to plummet, and the raincoat that kept her clothes dry offered nothing to keep her warm. Annie hurried to the house, intending to grab a coat for herself and a blanket for April.

"Amanda!" she called at the back door, and stopped still, knowing there would be no answer.

Two sets of footprints, April's and Annie's, crossed the yard toward the barn.

A third set of prints, the smallest of them all, stamped a path through the mud toward the gate to the west pasture.

"No, no, *no!*" Annie yelled with frustration. Forgetting the ice freezing on her face, that her hands were numb and stiff as clubs, that she could hardly blink her eyes against the frigid wind, Annie followed Amanda's trail toward Raja's voice.

Through the open gate, across the field, Annie kept moving, not wondering why, knowing that April wouldn't hesitate to go after her beloved peafowl, and that Amanda would follow April to the ends of the earth.

The thunder of Apple Creek drowned out her thoughts. She stopped at the top of the hill, shaking so hard she could hardly stand, and stared in horror at the river charging by less than a dozen feet below. Even as she shrank from the raging torrent, the plea rose above the din.

"Help! Help! *Aaaaaaagh!*"

The trees that grew on the banks of Apple Creek were submerged but for the uppermost branches. Raja and Rani perched precariously among the spindly twigs, fighting to keep their balance in the midst of the churning river as ice crystals formed on their feathers.

April, wearing her hooded winter coat and gloves, stood with the toes of her boots in the water, calling to the birds. Though they trusted April completely, Annie could feel their fear of the storm.

Amanda stood higher on the bank, watching her sister, her gloved hands folded before her face as if in prayer.

The peahen flew from the tree toward April, but a gust of wind caught the bird and dashed her into the floodwater. Rani screamed one desperate cry for help before she disappeared under the violently churning river.

"Rani! Raja, no!" April cried, but Raja shrieked in anguish and followed his mate into the water. Both birds were lost in the muddy roil that ripped at them, pulled them under, carried them swiftly away.

"April!" Annie screamed, knowing even as she stumbled

toward her daughters that she was too late, too late to stop April from doing what she knew her daughter was going to do, had to do, wouldn't consider not doing, and life proceeded in slow motion as April ran along the slope and leaped into the frigid, merciless waters after her friends.

"Amanda," Annie begged, as her practical, sensible, predictable daughter threw herself into the river in April's wake.

"Don't go," she breathed, but they were already gone. "Come back," she whimpered, but the flood galloped away with its riders and would not, could not, reverse direction.

She staggered forward. She would go in after them. But strong hands gripped her from behind, strong arms surrounded her, a strong spirit soothed her as a strong presence warmed her shaking limbs by drawing her inside his coat against his body.

"Bryan! Oh, God, Bryan! Help me, help me, please, please help me! I can't lose my girls, I can't, I can't, I can't." Annie sobbed. "They're all I have left. Please help me!"

The cold faded. Weary, so weary; if Annie could only close her eyes for a moment, perhaps she would fall asleep and not wake up again until she opened her eyes in Heaven. She sighed deeply. Drew awaited her there. April and Amanda would be there, no doubt with their arms around two aristocratic peafowl.

Annie coughed and winced at the rawness of her throat. She frowned, refusing to open her eyes and trying to remember why she was so determined to keep them closed.

"Mom. It's us. We're here. We're okay. I know you are awake. Open your eyes and talk to us."

Annie opened her eyes wide and sat up straight at April's directive. Cried out and threw her arms around her daughters and held them, held them tight.

"What happened?" she demanded. "What −" She sat back, still holding onto her girls, and realized she was lying in a hospital bed.

Bryan sat in a chair beside her bed, and she found herself

suspended in the clarity of his compelling gaze. His eyes were hazel, she thought, first golden, then green, now tinted aqua as the light played across his expression.

He held a pair of peacock feathers.

"You have pneumonia," he told Annie. "You've been here since Saturday." He answered her dazed expression. "It's Monday morning."

So many questions she wanted to ask, so many details she needed to know. But first, she turned to April. "I'm so sorry, honey, about Raja and Rani. I saw what happened to them."

"But they're okay, Mom! About one hundred yards from where we went into the water, the river was choked with debris. Raja and Rani got caught in it, and Amanda and I were able to grab onto the branches. We climbed out and pulled the birds up onto the bank. Firefighters came and got all four of us in a utility vehicle, and they dropped Raja and Rani off at Mr. English's house on the way to meet the ambulance that brought us here."

"By that time, you were already here," Bryan said. "And you were in worse shape than the girls. Despite their dip in the water, they were dressed for the weather. You were wearing a raincoat over a tee shirt and rubber boots over thin socks. The toes on your right foot are mildly frostbitten. You're fortunate it wasn't a lot worse."

"How did you know," Annie whispered. "How did you know we needed you?"

"The storms developed before the levees were completed, and the whole area flooded. I had to stop and check on you. I had to know that you and the girls were all right." Bryan studied the feathers in the dim light. "I saw the damage to your barn and outbuildings, and I radioed for a rescue squad and an ambulance. The back door of your house was open. Samson and Soleil were yowling at the storm door, looking toward the field. I saw your footprints in the mud and heard Raja calling for help. We responded as quickly as we could."

"Mr. English says Raja and Rani are going to be fine," April added. "He dried them and warmed them and gave them something to prevent respiratory infections. He will keep them confined at his place until we get a new shed and pen built. Then they can come home."

"Raja and Rani asked me to bring these to you." Bryan presented the feathers to Annie.

"They wanted you to have them," April said.

"And when did they tell you that?" Annie wanted to know.

"Rani wanted cat food last night. Bryan drove me to Mr. English's house so I could give her some. I gave her and Raja a whole scoop, and they gave me their feathers."

"Peacocks are sacred in certain cultures," Bryan said reverently, "for the all-seeing eyes in their feathers. The peacock represents a pure soul that cannot be corrupted." He glanced at April. "They are also believed to represent immortality and resurrection."

Perhaps this was why he understood April so well, Annie thought. Like her, Bryan had nothing to hide. April didn't recognize boundaries. Limitations. Impossibilities. Bryan recognized them, but chose to ignore them. He knew April could do anything, and he delighted in encouraging her to try.

"Who has taken care of the girls since Saturday?" Annie asked.

"Bryan brought Gina to stay with us when he drove us home from the hospital Saturday evening," Amanda said. "Gina loves cats, and she's really pretty! She braided April's hair and polished my nails. See?"

Annie complimented the perfectly applied coral-colored polish on Amanda's small fingernails.

"Gina says it sets off my blue eyes and dark hair," Amanda explained proudly. "She even brought April a hair clip shaped like Raja, and she gave me a painting of two cats sitting on a tree branch in the moonlight. It has a Bible verse on it. Bryan hung it on the wall beside my bed for me."

Annie looked Bryan in the eye, and this time she allowed him to see all the way into her heart. "Thank you," she said.

Bryan took her hand in both of his and said with a smile more than words could ever convey.

The third day of April faded into evening, though the sun still shone bright across the back yard as the girls waved goodbye to friends who had attended their birthday party.

"Eleven and nine," Bryan said. "You ladies are growing up fast. What is it like to share a birthday?"

"It's perfect!" April laughed.

"Perfect," Amanda agreed with a smile.

Bryan helped Annie break down the tent and the tables and put away the remaining party decorations. When they were finished, Annie invited him to join her in the kitchen for a slab of leftover birthday cake. She stepped out the back door to call April and Amanda inside, but the girls were missing.

She strolled down the lane to the reconstructed barn, smiling toward her garden shed on the way. Bryan and his friends had built it for her, customized as she had requested. A shout from April drew her attention to the field behind the barn, and Annie's breath caught in her throat.

Raja and Rani strutted along the top rail of the wood fence, followed by April and Amanda. The girls held their arms outstretched as though they walked a tightrope.

"April! Amanda! Get down from there, this instant!"

"It's okay, Mom! God's got me!" April leaped off the fence and ran, laughing, into the sunset.

Amanda dropped to the ground in pursuit of her sister, but turned after only a few steps and smiled back at Annie. "It's okay, Mom. God's got you, too. You are free to run and play like us. You don't have to hold your breath anymore."

Bryan joined Annie at the gate and draped his arm around her shoulders as the peafowl fluttered off the fence and hurried after the girls.

Annie marveled at herself and her children and other acts of God as she watched April chase the wind.

With Becky Lynn's Consent

Rape wasn't a word that was ever said where I grew up. It was generally figured that women wanted it even when they acted like they didn't, because after all, that's the way babies was made, and that's what women were put here for in the first place. If a man lost control of himself around a pretty woman, that surely wasn't his fault, and if she'd been more discreet about herself, it never would've happened. Nobody ever considered nothing about forcing a woman to do a thing against her will, 'cause a woman didn't have a will to force. I was raised by them rules and believed 'em to be right and proper. I never thought the creed I'd lived by all my life might be questionable or even wrong in some ways until all that happened with Becky Lynn.

I was seventeen that summer, stout and strong and brown from digging postholes to build Pap's new fence. I didn't have no use for girls. I'd not been around them to speak of, but from what Pap told me, they couldn't do much of anything, didn't have a lick of sense, and the stuff they did love to do, cooking and cleaning and raising babies and such, was boring beyond anything else I could imagine, even digging postholes. So when Pap told me it was time I consider taking a wife, I thought he'd done took leave of his senses.

Mama died when I was six years old. She was trying to push out my baby sister and wasn't strong enough to do it. The doctor went ahead and pulled the baby out of Mama's belly while Mama screamed so loud I could hear her clear out to the woodpile. Mama died then, and Pap didn't want the baby 'cause it was a girl and he didn't know what to do with one. The doctor said he knew a place that was good enough for it, and he wrapped it in a grass sack and put it on the floorboard of his old Ford pickup and drove off across the hill. I asked Pap one time what happened to my sister, and he told me it didn't matter, but he hoped it was something awful because she killed my mama, and he told me not to ever bring it up again, and I didn't, because he scared me.

We buried Mama in the middle of a stand of sycamore trees 'way up on the hill behind the house. Pap never went back up there to see the grave, and by the next summer when grass grew over everything, I'd forgotten exactly where it was, anyway.

I missed all the things Mama did for us more than I missed Mama. Pap wouldn't let her touch me much 'cause too much coddling turns a strong boy into a weak man, and I don't remember seeing Pap touch Mama but to push her out of his way now and again. It was odd how Pap quieted down after Mama died. Once in a while I'd catch him staring off toward the sycamores on the hill, and I wondered if maybe in his own way he cared more for Mama than he would ever admit.

The lack of a woman made for some problems. Pap couldn't cook and it was beneath him to try, so he went into town and hired a wretched old widow woman to cook supper for us. The doctor had to drive by our place on his way home every night, so he'd drop off whatever she'd fixed, and we'd give him the dishes from the day before to take back. We never washed 'em. That was woman's work, Pap said. We'd eat our supper and save the leftovers for breakfast the next morning. We never had lunch 'cause we were too busy and because we had eaten all the food by then, anyway.

Once in a while Pap would shoot a rabbit or a few squirrels and give them to the doctor to take to the widow woman along with her pay. I never understood why he would do a nice thing like that when he always talked about how undeserving she was and how the good Lord proved it by taking her husband away when they were both young. Pap said it was because the husband had been too gentle with his wife, let her be too happy and feel too free, let her forget her proper place. She was going to have a baby when her husband died, Pap said. I wondered whatever happened to it, but I was scared to ask.

The widow woman was still cooking for us the summer I was seventeen. I was going to be eighteen in the fall and never really give much thought to the future. Pap took me out of school after the third grade to help with the farm, and I just figured I'd spend the rest of my life right there, tending the hogs and working the fields. But Pap said while I had no need of a fancy education, I would have need of a woman. That widow wouldn't cook for us forever, she was gonna die one of these days, and I should find me a hearty young woman to sew and cook and clean and raise up a son to fill my shoes, just like Mama had done for Pap.

Don't look in town for a wife, Pap said, 'cause the women there were starting to get ideas about having rights and deciding things for themselves. It was because their parents let them go to school, Pap said, and they got an education and learned too much about things a woman didn't need to know nothing about in the first place. Look in the hills, he said, for a quiet girl who minded her own pap to the letter and could be brought home for the price of a good fattening hog. That sounded right to me, and that's what I meant to do.

The first lesson I learned that summer, really learned for myself instead of having it told to me, is that you won't always do what you mean to do, no matter how fiercely you mean to do it. Sometimes things just turn out different and there's not a thing you can do but sit there and watch.

It started when Pap fell through the roof of our house. It wasn't nothing more than a shack, really, and had been falling apart for as long as I could remember, but the roof started leaking real bad right above Pap's bed, so he decided to climb up there with a good-sized square of rusty tin and at least redirect the flow to a different corner of the house. He was nailing it in place good and strong when the whole roof gave way and collapsed. Bad thing was, Pap kept going right on through the floor into the cellar below.

I was slopping hogs when I heard the sounds, the splintering wood, the momentary suspension like a moth's first brush against a spider's web, then the crash, not hard and fast, but slow and deliberate, like each piece knew exactly where it was supposed to fall. I just stood there with all these helpless thoughts stampeding through my mind and then, just before the final *whump*, I heard Pap yell, and he sounded little and far away, and I felt like I was going to be sick.

I threw down the bucket and ran up the holler to the house, but there was nothing to see but a pile of rotted timbers that wouldn't've even made good firewood, with spindly scraps of tin sprouting up here and there still dancing around from the commotion, like they was happy they no longer had to pretend to serve a purpose they hadn't served for years.

Pap yelled again, and I climbed in among all the stuff until I could look down into the cellar and see him lying there, covered with dirt and rubbish. A piece of rusty tin, maybe the one he had been trying to nail down, was embedded over halfway through his left thigh, and blood was pumping rhythmically out around it, washing dirt and Pap's life away in its thick, dark flow. I screamed that I was going for the doctor, and Pap said not to hurry, it didn't hurt none, but his lips were blue and he already looked as good as dead, and I jumped on our old mule and whipped it harder and stronger than Pap ever did all the way to the doctor's house. We got in his truck and drove right back to the farm, and his three boys with us. They were younger than me, but good stout fellows, and we lowered the youngest down to Pap, and he tied ropes around Pap's ankles and chest, and we pulled Pap out of the ground with that piece of tin still in his leg. When we got him on level ground we could see there wasn't anything holding Pap's leg on but a little sliver of meat, and when the doctor yanked out that piece of tin and Pap's leg came off with it, I ran behind the woodpile and vomited so hard I almost passed out.

The doctor fixed Pap up as best he could there on the ground, then him and his boys stuffed Pap in that old Ford, and the doctor drove for an hour to Statler Ridge and left Pap in the hospital there. I stayed the night at the doctor's house and wondered if Pap was still alive, and wondered if prayer would help, as if I knew how to pray, because while Pap mentioned people that the Lord punished ever so often, he never explained much else about Him.

The doctor kept me at his house for the next week. I rode the mule home every morning and worked our farm all day to keep things up as best I could until Pap was able to come back. Doc called Statler Ridge from his office every afternoon to check on Pap, and on the fifth day he came back from town earlier than usual and stopped by the farm to talk to me before he went home.

Pap wasn't gonna walk no more, he said, not just because he was missing a leg, but because his back had been injured when he fell. Wasn't nothing no doctor in the world could do to fix that. Pap would be out of the hospital in a couple more weeks, and they was fixin' to get him a wheelchair to get around in, but he wouldn't be able to come back up to the hills, Doc said, and I knew he was right. Pap and me didn't even have a house no more, and Pap couldn't help me farm if he couldn't even stand up. We'd have to live in town, Doc said.

I hated that thought 'bout as much as I ever hated anything, and I felt lost as a boy ever did when Doc offered to buy the farm from me, hogs and all, for a decent price so Pap and I could afford to live in town. He give me some more things to think about before he got in that old truck and chugged on up the hill to his own place.

Turns out the wretched old widow woman Pap had talked about for years wasn't so old after all, more like Pap's age, and not wretched at all but pretty decent, though maybe too smart for her own good.

Doc said a long time ago young Mathias Johnson left town for four years and came back with a college degree and Mrs. Johnson.

They opened a boarding house, which did right well until the state built roads that routed traffic past the town instead of through it, which suited all the locals just fine, on account that it discouraged outsiders from visiting with interfering ideas. Doc said Mr. Johnson tried to convince people to open new businesses and bring progress to the area, but local folks didn't have enough spending money to support new businesses, and if they did they would've kept it in their pockets, 'cause they weren't interested in the kind of progress Mr. Johnson had learned about during his four years in the big city. Doc said nobody was real broke up when Mr. Johnson died, though they thought it a shame he should come to such an end. They all thought Mrs. Johnson would pack up and go back to wherever she came from after she was widowed, but she didn't, and she continued to run the boarding house all by herself, though it could hardly be called that now, Doc said, 'cause Mrs. Johnson hadn't put up any visitors for a long time.

Doc talked her into renting us a couple of rooms indefinitely. He said Mrs. Johnson lived shamefully unfettered because no self-respecting man would have her with her independent ways, so I'd have keep my own counsel in deciding what allowances to make for her behavior and how to set my foot down if it became necessary to assert control of a situation.

Doc said she'd let us build a ramp along her back steps for Pap's wheelchair, and she'd continue to cook for us, too. That part did appeal to me, 'cause since Mama died, I hadn't lived with a woman until I stayed with the doctor and his wife, and it sure was nice to sit down to a hot meal that was fresh cooked, instead of eating lukewarm vegetables and stale bread. Doc and his boys always wore clean clothes, too, and theirs weren't full of holes. I could get used to that.

Doc said he didn't see as how Pap and me had a choice in the matter, and when he went and got Pap from Statler Ridge and I met them at the boarding house, I could see he was right. Something had gone out of Pap. I tried to talk to him about selling the home place, but he didn't seem to care about anything. Doc gave me the money that afternoon, and I was officially a city boy.

I didn't know how to act around Mrs. Johnson, 'cause no woman had ever really talked straight to me before. I was suspicious of her at first, in keeping with my raising, but I was surprised right off to find out that she was just a person, like me and Pap, and if she was different in some ways, at least they weren't bad ways. Mrs. Johnson helped me and Doc get Pap settled into the bed in his new room, and she brought some homemade vegetable soup, and when Pap wouldn't even lift a finger to eat it, Mrs. Johnson sat down right on the edge of the bed with Pap and spooned that food into his mouth. I was shocked, not only 'cause Pap didn't object to her being there, but because he ate every bite she gave him and drank down a whole mug of milk.

We left Pap alone to sleep then, and Doc went on home, and Mrs. Johnson said I needed stronger food than Pap because I wasn't recovering from anything, and she set me down in front of a big ol' slab of ham, a plate full of roastin' ears, bowls of mashed potatoes and butter beans, and biscuits the size of my fist. I don't recall ever eating so much in my life up to that point, nor do I recall thanking anybody for anything, but it seemed the proper thing to do after all that food I put away. Mrs. Johnson just smiled and mentioned that there was a pump and a bucket in front of the shed out back, and a metal tub inside that shed, if I had a mind to wash up. She handed me a cake of lye soap before I could answer, but considerin' I hadn't washed like that since Mama died, I decided to go ahead and do that, too. Mrs. Johnson had prepared ahead of time, not only for Pap's arrival, but also for mine. She handed me a fresh shirt and pants one of the neighbors had given her for me, and I put them on after I had washed myself, and I must admit, that felt pretty good.

That started me to thinking that maybe Pap was right, that it was time to get me a wife who could treat me like that all the time. A girl from the hills, Pap had said, and that night I started planning a trip, starting from Doc's place and going on up into the mountains. It might take me a few weeks. I knew of several farmers along through there who had daughters, but I didn't want to settle for the first one I came across.

And then I started thinking about other things that made me a mite uncomfortable. Pap had no use at all for women from town, because he thought they were too spirited, too bent on independence. But I liked the way Mrs. Johnson smiled and laughed and talked right out loud like it was okay for her to. The few women I could recall from the hills rarely smiled, never laughed, and if they spoke out loud it was with their heads and eyes lowered, like they expected to be slapped down for daring to open their mouths. Being around Mrs. Johnson just for a few hours that afternoon made me wonder why it was so bad for a woman to have a little life about her. Mrs. Johnson was more like a companion than a burden, and she certainly wasn't useless or weak, and she was actually pretty smart about the things we talked about. I tossed and turned for hours in the unfamiliarity of my new life, and by the time I fell asleep, I had decided to postpone my wife-hunting trip for a few weeks. The next morning I was glad I did.

The next morning I met Becky Lynn.

Becky Lynn Johnson was the baby the wretched old widow woman was carrying when her husband was gored to death by a bull. Becky Lynn was eight months younger than me, and from the moment I laid eyes on her, I never saw another thing.

I slept later than I ever had the next morning, and by the time I jumped out of bed and dressed and hurried to the kitchen, Mrs. Johnson had already fed Pap his breakfast and was beginning preparations for lunch. She had kept eggs and ham and biscuits hot for me, and I ate to the staccato beat of axe meeting wood in Mrs. Johnson's back yard. When I finished, I mumbled my thanks to her quiet smile and visited Pap in his room.

Pap had the benefit of a window from which he could see the neighbor's shed or, if he leaned sideways in his bed, the street in front of Mrs. Johnson's house. The yard between the window and the shed was usually occupied by Mrs. Johnson's chickens, the neighbor's goats, or someone else's dog that happened by to chase everything else away.

Pap was staring out that window when I entered his room. He didn't answer when I talked to him, even when I urged him to let me help him into his new wheelchair so I could take him out into the sunshine. When I took hold of his arm, thinking maybe I'd put him in the chair anyway, he jerked away and swore at me and told me to leave him alone. I left him glaring out the window at an enemy only he could see.

I was missing my pocket watch, the only thing I'd brought away from the home place. It had belonged to Mama's Pap, and she had kept it in a little satin-lined box in a dresser drawer. She would take it out now and then and look at it and sigh real deep and put it away again. Pap never touched it before Mama died and never took it out of the drawer afterwards. Before I sold the place to Doc, I looked over the rubble that had been our house to see if there was anything worth the trouble of picking up, when I recognized the dresser, broke all to pieces where it had stood by itself against one corner. I moved the pieces aside and there was that little box lying on the ground, just waiting for somebody to find it. The watch inside wasn't hurt a bit, and it still run when I wound the stem. I dropped it in my pocket and took it back to town. I never mentioned it to Pap. Somehow I didn't think he would like knowing I was carrying something that had meant so much to Mama.

The watch had been in the pocket of my pants when I washed up the night before, and I had left my old clothes out in the shed because they smelled too bad to bring back inside. When I left Pap that morning, I went out the back door to go and get my watch. I glanced toward the woodpile to see who was doing such a steady, earnest job with that axe, and there she was: Becky Lynn.

She was wearing denim pants and a work shirt with the sleeves rolled up. Heavy gloves protected hands that I soon learned were both delicate and strong. Hair the color of autumn wheat was tied back with a shoestring, and little strands had escaped to curl against the dampness on her face. She swung that axe with skill born of years of experience, splitting wood into kindling as good as any man I had ever seen.

After a little bit she caught sight of me out of the corner of her eye and turned to look straight at me, no doubt wondering who I was and what I was doing just standing there. I'd never looked into eyes so blue, and I stared all the more because she had the prettiest face I'd ever seen. She turned and swung the axe into a chunk as big as a tree stump and walked right over to me, pulling off her right glove. She said I must be Will Daugherty, and she offered a hand for me to shake and smiled her mother's smile.

Her hand was soft and small, but with a firm, honest grip. She looked me right in the face and talked to me like she'd known me forever, and I felt like I was standing with my equal, not with a weak, dumb girl. And I liked her. No, I loved her. From that moment forward, I was hopelessly in love with Becky Lynn Johnson.

She liked, me, too, although she was a little wary at first. I never tried to take her jobs away from her, but I started pitching in, helping chop wood and hoe the garden and feed and milk the handful of cows Mrs. Johnson kept in the little field behind the shed. I got to know Becky Lynn real well, and decided pretty quick that all the things Pap had ever told me about women must be, if not wrong, just not about women like Mrs. Johnson and Becky Lynn. Problem was, I still had a lot to learn.

One thing I soon learned is that local men felt pretty much the same way Pap did about women keeping their place. If Pap didn't want me to marry a woman from town because he thought they were all like the wretched widow woman, he was wrong, 'cause there wasn't much difference between them and the women up in the hills. As I got out and met more people, it didn't take long to realize that Mrs. Johnson and Becky Lynn were about the only women I ever caught with smiles on their faces. They looked genuinely happy. Other women I saw in town looked like their faces were carved from stone, hard and miserable and unyielding, like Doc's wife, like my mama. Though Mrs. Johnson's wild ideas about women being equal to men and deserving of an education and their own income didn't earn her any friends, the menfolk didn't do anything to stop her beyond making sure her outlandish notions didn't spread any farther than her own doorstep. They managed their own women in their own homes, and Mrs. Johnson was left to spinsterhood along with her daughter, 'cause neither of them was submissive as becomes any woman hoping to be considered a proper wife.

I learned that it was a rite of passage for a boy to find himself a pretty young girl and take her out somewhere and knock her up. I learned that girls who resisted got persuaded with slaps and punches. I learned that girls who cried about it later got hushed by their mamas and switched by their papas for being easy. Boys were just giving in to their natural inclinations. Girls were asking for it, how I never quite figured out, except I guess just because they happened to be girls. All a boy had to say is that the girl gave her consent for him to have his way with her, and all the men would believe him, and the girl would see that it was useless to claim she had been forced. She would close her mouth and lock the horror and fear and shame away inside herself and her face would begin to harden until, years later, she couldn't remember what it had ever been like to smile.

I learned all that and more in the first three months Pap and me lived at the Johnson place. I also knew there was talk that me and Becky Lynn were already considered a couple. When my eighteenth birthday rolled around in October and Becky Lynn baked me a cake, it was considered official. That was fine with me, and by then it was fine with Becky Lynn, too.

We worked together every day and studied our lessons side by side. Girls didn't go to school beyond the eighth grade because that was the most schooling girls were thought to need. Mrs. Johnson called that line of thinking backward, but she didn't want Becky Lynn to be the only girl in a roomful of high school boys, so she continued her daughter's schooling at home. When I mentioned my lack of learning, Mrs. Johnson looked at me with genuine pity in her eyes, and I was embarrassed, 'cause nobody'd ever showed me sympathy about nothing before, not even when Mama died.

Mrs. Johnson saw to my education along with Becky Lynn's that fall. One whole wall of her parlor was lined floor to ceiling with shelves full of books. Mrs. Johnson taught me to read, not just words I'd never heard before, but poetry and literature and hymns that made speaking something to enjoy and not just a means to an end. Every time I opened a book, I learned about other worlds far beyond the boundaries of what little I knew, and that these places weren't necessarily bad just because they happened to be different. I felt something then that I'd never felt before, sort of a pang that what I had wasn't nearly all there was, and my heart hurt with a yearning to see and touch and taste some of the places and things I read about in Mrs. Johnson's books.

In the evenings when work and schooling were done, me and Becky Lynn would go riding on the neighbor's horses or fishing in the pond on the other side of the holler or just walk in the cool of the wood. On the evening of my eighteenth birthday I told Becky Lynn I loved her, and she said she loved me, too, and we kissed for the first time right there in the woods, and I felt like I had the whole world in my arms when she pressed herself against me. We sat on the moss beneath a big old tree and talked about the future until 'way after dark, and when we went home I got the first disapproving look from Mrs. Johnson that she had ever sent my way, and I was surprised at how much it hurt.

The morning after my birthday I went out early and carved mine and Becky Lynn's initials in a heart on that big old tree. That afternoon I learned that I wasn't the only one with plans for Becky Lynn.

Clete Parker stood over six feet tall and must've been close to three hundred pounds. He was both fat and muscular, the way some farm boys are just plain big all over. He could lift more, push harder, and pull farther than any other man in town, and he spent most of his waking hours telling everybody about it. He also drank a little, never a lot, because a little is all it took to turn the braggart into a raging bull. I had only seen Clete drunk a few times. He found trouble then wherever he looked, and nobody else was big enough or brave enough to get in his way when he felt the need to destroy its source. Clete had run afoul of the law when he went out to conquer the world. Folks in other places took exception to the things he got away with at home, and Clete spent two years in a little square room made of concrete blocks and iron bars for sins he never got around to confessing after he got out and hightailed it home. Folks generally regarded Clete as a blowhard spoiling for a fight, to be tolerated agreeably lest he imagine offense and break the offender in two. Truth was, their pacifyin' concessions were lame excuses to let him be, 'cause everybody was afraid of Clete. None of the men would dare cross him, 'cause each knew that he'd find himself facing Clete alone before an audience that would stand by and let fate take its course before stepping in to collect his remains.

Clete knew he was safe within the confines of his community because he had everybody running scared and laws, such as they were, didn't apply to him here. The hollers and hills and the few flat acres we called a town existed within the blessing and curse of isolation. Larger towns lay miles distant and worlds apart, and folks with definite ideas of what constituted civilization turned a blind eye to what they considered beneath their notice.

The men had stronger reasons than cowardice to stay on Clete's good side. None was willing to appear less tough and unyielding than the next man lest he be accused of becoming lax like Mr. Johnson, whose name had become a real insult over the years. What nobody recognized from their shadows of self-preservation was that Clete meant to make somebody sorry for his outrage over his imprisonment. He was trying to provoke a conflict so he could feel justified in doing some damage, but when folks acquiesced to his brutality for fear of incurring his wrath if they didn't, his need for vengeance went unsatisfied and simmered all the hotter deep down inside where such things mattered. Folks tolerated Clete's drinking and brawling much as they put up with Mrs. Johnson, figuring both fires would eventually burn out on their own if everybody just ignored them and took care not to add any fuel.

Clete didn't need liquor to know that whatever he wanted was his for the taking. And he wanted Becky Lynn Johnson. Rules of etiquette, such as they were, decreed that if a girl already belonged to somebody else in a soon-to-be-permanent fashion, it was ungentleman-like to interfere and go messing with another man's claim. It was no secret that Becky Lynn was my girl. But Clete wasn't one to let morals get in his way. He let the town know, and me with it, that Becky Lynn wasn't going to get away with merely baking him a cake when his next birthday came along.

The week before Thanksgiving Mr. Floyd hired me to help out part time around the general store. I was glad of the work and the money, since I knew what Doc had paid Pap and me for the farm wouldn't last forever, and I was going to need a substantial savings, because I was going to ask Becky Lynn to marry me in the spring.

Clete always knew when I was going to be at the store for a few hours, because he would ask Mr. Floyd when I was supposed to be at work, and Mr. Floyd was too scared to hold out. Sometimes Clete would call on Mrs. Johnson while I was away and ask all kinds of questions about Becky Lynn while he sat at the kitchen table and ate them out of house and home. Other times he would follow me around the store as I cleaned up or stocked shelves and make obscene comments about my relationship with Becky Lynn and get mad because I wouldn't verify any of his conjectures. A few times he tried to get fresh with Becky Lynn, but she always managed to slip away before he got over himself enough to realize she was gone.

I put up with Clete like everybody else did and took for granted that he would soon tire of his futile pursuit and find another girl to chase. He often bragged about previous exploits with a multitude of young women, counting notches on his belt as he called their names. I figured that's all he thought Becky Lynn amounted to – another notch on that belt. I figured wrong. Becky Lynn was the prettiest girl, the one who smiled without fear, the one who most aroused his desire to overpower the free spirit that ever danced just beyond his reach. He knew that with the possible of exception of me, no man had ever had Becky Lynn, and he wanted to be the first to break her in.

Maybe part of the reason I found it so easy to brush off Clete's advances toward Becky Lynn is that I was dealing with what I thought were more serious problems at the time. Pap still wouldn't eat unless Mrs. Johnson sat down and fed him like a child. He wouldn't wash himself, and Mrs. Johnson was only willing to go so far with a pan of water and a soapy cloth. He wouldn't get out of bed, and he fought anybody who tried to force him, throwing his fists and swearing like a madman. He wouldn't talk to anybody, not even Doc, who had been his friend for longer than I had lived.

Mrs. Johnson left a pail and a towel beside the bed for Pap's toilet. How he managed we never knew, for he always answered the call of nature when none of us was around. I emptied the pail a couple of times a day, 'cause I figured Mrs. Johnson did enough for Pap and shouldn't have to handle such an unfriendly task for such an ungrateful person.

Once every couple of weeks Doc would come by with his boys, and the lot of us would haul Pap out of bed and set him on the floor – he'd fight like the devil if we tried to put him in that wheelchair – so Mrs. Johnson could change the bed linens. Other than that, Pap refused to move, and none of us knew how to make him. He shriveled a little more every day, despite Mrs. Johnson's good feeding, and his skin got white and pasty, like a real old person's who's been sick to death, but Pap wasn't real old and hadn't really been sick. He just went and give up, Doc said, and there's not much that can be done to help somebody who don't have the gumption to help himself.

That Christmas was the most beautiful time of my entire life, and to this day I wish the good Lord would've seen fit to just end my life right then and there, when I was happy and life was as good as it was ever going to be.

I'd never experienced a real Christmas. Becky Lynn took me tree hunting the week before the big day, and when she found just the right one, I cut it down and dragged it back to the house. I helped Mrs. Johnson brace it up in the corner of the parlor, and I sat on the bench in front of the old upright piano and ate gingerbread cookies and drank hot, spicy cider while they arranged homemade ornaments all over that tree. The only storebought decoration was a shiny silver star that I had to put on top, because the women were too short to reach that high. It sure was a pretty sight when they got done. By then it was late, past the time I normally went to bed, but Mrs. Johnson sat down at the piano and started to play Christmas songs. I felt foolish at first 'cause I'd never even heard the songs they were singing, never heard many songs at all as a matter of fact, but they pulled me right in and taught me the words, and I learned that I had a pretty fair voice for making music.

That Christmas I used some of my very own earnings to buy some material I had seen Mrs. Johnson admiring in the mercantile. It cost more than she had been willing to spend, and the look on her face when she tore back the paper and caressed that soft fabric, the same blue as her eyes, made me feel big and important like I'd never felt before, as if I'd done something special that really mattered.

I bought a gold locket on a chain for Becky Lynn. I felt real awkward watching her open it, hoping like crazy she'd like it, 'cause I'd never bought a gift for a girl before. It was shaped like a book, and she put a little picture of her mama on one side, and an old picture of her papa on the other, and then she just held it open and looked at it for the longest time, like she was holding the most precious treasure in the world.

I got Pap a tin of his favorite tobacco, 'cause he'd always loved a good chaw, and he hadn't had any since we moved to town back in the summer, so I thought maybe a gift like that would remind him of better times and maybe help him enjoy the time he had right here and now. But Pap didn't acknowledge or accept or enjoy my present. I tried to talk to him, went on and on about the decorations and the food and the tree, but he never turned his gaze away from that window, and I didn't think he heard so much as one word that I said. I finally set the tobacco on the bed beside him and left. After I closed the door I heard a crash. I went running back in with Mrs. Johnson right behind me, and sure enough, Pap had hurled that tin of tobacco clear across the room, where it broke one of Mrs. Johnson's pretty lamps.

He was just lying there like I'd left him, staring out that window as if he'd never moved, except I saw a tear, a real tear mind you, making its unfamiliar way down beside Pap's nose, and he swallowed loud enough for all of us to hear. Mrs. Johnson didn't notice because she was too busy picking up the pieces of her lamp, and I figured maybe it would embarrass Pap if I said anything, 'cause I'd never seen any sign of weakness in him ever before now, and I didn't want to make him any madder than he already was. So when Mrs. Johnson left the room with an apron full of broken glass and the tobacco tin, I followed her out and didn't go to see Pap again until the next day.

Christmas night I put on the shirt Becky Lynn had made for me and went with her and her mama to the little white church that perched just above the holler on the outskirts of town. The holler and the church were called Hazel Creek. I was eighteen years old and had never set foot in the door of a church before that night. The little kids put on a play about the birth of Jesus, and I felt just like one of them scared, helpless shepherds out in the field, learning about the Christ child for the first time. The adults read scriptures from the Bible, and I followed along as best I could in the one Mrs. Johnson had given me for a Christmas present.

My heart changed somehow that night. It wasn't like I got struck by lightning or the earth moved, more like a realization that I wasn't alone in the world after all, that even though Pap was waiting to die and mad that it was taking so long, the good Lord was still watching out for us both and was always there if we needed Him. I'd heard people mention the Lord from time to time as I grew up, but never as a savior and a friend. It was nice to have finally met Him for myself.

When we got home Christmas night it was late, and I had to

really beg Mrs. Johnson to let me take Becky Lynn for a walk in the moonlight, just a real quick short one, and she finally agreed, saying she was going to time me, and I'd better have Becky Lynn home when I promised I would.

I took Becky Lynn down to our tree in the woods and told her I loved her and asked her to marry me. She didn't hesitate to say yes, and flung herself in my arms, and I worked my hands in under her coat and warmed them against the material that separated them from the small of her back. We talked all the way back to the house and told Mrs. Johnson, who smiled like she'd known all along, and we sat in the kitchen and drank hot cider and started setting down plans to make it official in the spring.

First I wanted to buy Becky Lynn a real engagement ring. Few of the girls in our area got one, most never even got a wedding band, but it was important to me that Becky Lynn have both. I'd have enough money saved in another month or two, but Becky Lynn said she didn't care about the ring, it was enough to know she was going to be my wife, and we were so happy that we laughed right out loud at everything and nothing. Like I said before, I wish the good Lord would've seen fit to just take me out right then, that night, when life was perfect and love meant everything and happiness felt like a promise that would never go away.

The week after Christmas things got back to normal around town. Clete Parker made a comment or two about how he'd never gotten around to giving Becky Lynn the Christmas present he was saving for her, and I told him he was too late anyway 'cause she was going to be my wife, and he stomped out of the store and we didn't see him for the rest of the week.

The day before New Year's I bought some popcorn and fruit Mrs. Johnson had asked for. As I paid for the stuff, I noticed Mr. Floyd acting real squirrelly, downright nervous, and when I asked him what was the matter, he nearly fell over himself trying to tell me it wasn't his fault, Clete threatened to kill him if he told, and it wasn't none of his business anyway 'cause all that was between me and Clete. I finally pinned him down to an explanation, and he told me Clete had gone to the Johnson place for a date with Becky Lynn, but I wasn't supposed to know about it. When I snorted and said Becky Lynn wouldn't be caught dead with Clete, Mr. Floyd said it didn't matter what Becky Lynn wanted 'cause she was just a girl and Clete was a man, and it wouldn't hurt her none to be brought down a notch or two, though it was a shame that such a pretty girl should wind up with the likes of Clete, and I felt a cold, hard knot forming in the pit of my stomach like I'd never felt before, not even when Pap came back from Statler Ridge missing more than a leg.

I left the stuff I'd already paid for sitting on Mr. Floyd's counter and ran faster than I knew I could all the way home. When I charged into the kitchen, I knew I was already too late.

Mrs. Johnson sat at the table sobbing into a handkerchief, and one of her eyes was purple and swollen shut. I didn't have to ask what had happened, but I did ask where he had taken Becky Lynn. Mrs. Johnson cried that she didn't know. Clete had dragged Becky Lynn out to his truck and shoved her inside, kicking and screaming and begging to be let go. Turned out, that had been almost two hours ago.

I forced myself to think, trying to decide what to do, 'cause Mrs. Johnson didn't have a car, but I could take one of the neighbor's horses and check out some of the places I'd heard the men tell tales about, and I could sure enough carry a gun. That hadn't much more than crossed my mind when we heard a sickening thud by the back door.

Mrs. Johnson got there first and flung it open. Becky Lynn fell inside, crawled into her mama's arms, and cried like I'd never heard anybody cry before. They just sat there on the floor together and held each other and sobbed while I stood by helpless and angry and knowing nothing I could do would ever put things back the way they had been.

Mrs. Johnson finally drew back and tried to help her daughter stand up. Becky Lynn's face was a mess of purple bruises, her lips were busted and swollen, and blood had run down under her chin. Her dress was ripped up so badly it was hardly hanging on to her body and I saw scratches disappearing in the direction of her bosom. Both her shoes were gone. But the most horrifying thing, the thing that sent me over the edge, was when she stood up and I saw blood running down the insides of her legs mingled with streaks of white. She stood bowlegged and cried out when she tried to take a step toward the kitchen table. Becky Lynn had been a virgin. Now she was a victim, another notch on a long leather belt, and the anger that built up inside me drove me to a level of insanity I had never experienced before.

And I did the absolute worst thing a man could ever do to the woman he loves.

I took it all out on Becky Lynn.

How could you, I heard Pap's voice, not really aware that it was coming out of my mouth. We were going to be married! How could you go with him! How could you let him do this to you when you were supposed to belong to me! You promised, *you promised,* to stay faithful to me forever, and now you've gone and done this with Clete Parker, of all the men in the world...

My voice grew louder as my rage grew stronger, and Becky Lynn backed up against the cabinet and sank slowly to the floor, sobbing, with her forehead on her knees and her arms wrapped up over her head as though protecting herself from falling debris. All the things Pap had ever told me about women came back to haunt me. A man couldn't help following his inborn desires. If he got carried away with a pretty girl, that wasn't his fault, and if she'd have been more discreet about herself it never would've happened in the first place. And anyway, if a girl was that serious about not giving in, she could always fight the man off and walk away. It was that simple. You couldn't really call it force, when that's what women were put on this earth for anyway. Women just had a tendency to forget themselves in the heat of the moment, and then would carry on about it later because they realized they'd ruined their reputation by being so free and easy to begin with.

I shocked myself by yelling such hideous things at Becky Lynn. I wanted to stop, but I couldn't, I didn't know how, and the more I said, the more I hated myself for saying it, and the more I hated Pap for raising me to be like him.

Mrs. Johnson put an end to it. She walked up to me and slapped me hard right across the face, so hard that the sting brought tears to my eyes. I touched my face and looked into her eyes; they were filled with anger, sadness, and bitter, bitter disappointment that I could betray her daughter so viciously when she needed me the most. Mrs. Johnson told me to get out of her house.

I walked out the back door in slow motion and went and sat on the woodpile. It was cold and the air had a bite that numbed my lungs when I inhaled and then hurt, like I was breathing around the blade of a real sharp knife stuck deep in my gut.

Mrs. Johnson hollered at a neighbor, who went and got the sheriff and the doctor. They came to the house together and were inside for quite some time, and when they left they slapped each other on the back and chuckled knowingly, the way men do when they've gotten away with something.

I knew what would happen next. They'd go to the general store and wait for Clete to show up, early tomorrow if not this very evening, and he'd go into every vulgar detail of how he'd taken Becky Lynn, and then the doctor would exploit her injuries, and the sheriff would warn that Mrs. Johnson wanted to have Clete thrown in jail, and Clete would say, now you know I had Becky Lynn's consent or I never would've laid a hand on her.

I spend the night shivering on the woodpile, watching Mrs. Johnson move back and forth in front of the kitchen window as she tended her daughter's injuries. I prayed for forgiveness, from the good Lord if not from Mrs. Johnson, and when morning came I approached the back door and knocked as quiet and respectful as any visitor.

Mrs. Johnson's face crumbled when she saw me. She hadn't turned the light out all night long, hadn't went to bed, hadn't rested or slept. She had bore the burden of her daughter's rape all alone with neither help nor support from a single soul. It was more than she could handle.

I'd had enough as well. Her punishment, well deserved, had hurt more than I would have believed. She and Becky Lynn were family, especially since Pap was in such a bad way, and they were all I had in the world. I stood outside the screen door and looked at Mrs. Johnson and it hit me how much she'd been like a mama to me since Pap and me moved in, and I couldn't help it, I started to cry. I told her how sorry I was for everything, and how I hadn't meant any of those horrible things I said, and if she never forgave me I would understand.

It may just have been that Mrs. Johnson needed me even worse than I needed her, but I like to think that she accepted my apology and knew I meant it from the bottom of my heart. She opened the screen door and pulled me into the kitchen and put her arms around my neck and laid her head on my chest and cried until she had the hiccups. I sat her down and got a towel for her to wipe her face with and got her a glass of water. I said I was sorry again and asked what I could do to help.

Marry Becky Lynn, she said, in the spring like we had planned. Love Becky Lynn, and understand that none of this was her fault and that she was forced against her will and that she would never be the same because of it, but it would be a hundred times worse if I quit loving her, and Mrs. Johnson broke down and cried again.

She went to Becky Lynn's room and told her about my apology and that I still loved her and wanted to marry her. A few days later Becky Lynn allowed Mrs. Johnson to coax her out to the parlor, and I sat down beside Becky Lynn and told her all those things myself. She just looked at me, right through me. It would take her a while to forgive me, to trust me again, but she was willing to let me be her friend, and I was overjoyed with that.

I quit working for Mr. Floyd. It was too much to see all those patronizing faces lined up around the wood stove, just dying for me to say something about Clete and Becky Lynn. And though I wouldn't let Mrs. Johnson or Becky Lynn know for the world, I was having a hard time dealing with what had happened and with the fact that the whole town not only knew about it, but that folks were acting all self-righteous and smug and satisfied that Becky Lynn had been broken and shamed, as if they truly believed she had finally got what she deserved.

I was also worried about what might happen if I ever met up with Clete. Lord knows he could've crushed me without even trying, but if I started something and wound up in jail, I would leave Mrs. Johnson and Becky Lynn completely unprotected, and that scared me more than anything. That was the thought that really made me decide to quit working for Mr. Floyd. I could find steady work to do around the boarding house, and if it didn't make me no extra money, at least I could keep a constant eye on Becky Lynn and Mrs. Johnson.

Becky Lynn healed up faster on the outside than she did on the inside. She would smile simply because she knew I was trying so hard to make her smile, and then it was as if the very effort had worn her out. The smile would fade and she would look off into the distance for the longest time, and I wondered if she and Pap ever saw the same thing.

Clete Parker came by the last week of January. I was shoveling a clean white path from the house to the road when he came across the yard, wallowing out his own dirty tracks in the snow. He came straight for me and then stopped about a dozen feet away, roving his eyes over the piece at my waist. I was pleased that he took notice. Wearing a pistol had become second nature for me since New Year's Eve. Nobody would force his way into the house to blacken Mrs. Johnson's eye and take Becky Lynn away as long as I had the ability to stop him.

The pistol belonged to Pap. When Doc cleared away the remains of our home up in the hills, he came across Pap's shotgun and pistol and was nice enough to bring them to us. I let Doc keep the shotgun. There was plenty of ammo, too. I told Clete so and asked if he'd like to see a bullet for himself.

Clete told me he understood how I must feel, seeing how I had meant to marry Becky Lynn and then she went and threw herself at him, but hey, he was never one to turn down a lovesick girl. Sure he might've been a little rough, but that was okay with Becky

Lynn. He giggled, and I smelled the liquor on his breath.

No, it wasn't okay with Becky Lynn, I stated flatly. It wasn't okay with Mrs. Johnson. And it wasn't okay with me. I told him that if I could've fulfilled my fondest wish at that very moment, I'd've hogtied Clete and let Becky Lynn castrate him with a dull knife while the whole town watched, and then I'd've shot him dead right there in the snow. But I wanted to spend the rest of my life loving Becky Lynn more than I wanted to sit in a cell for killing Clete. So I told him to get off our property before I hauled off and did it anyway. And I told him to not ever come back.

If I surprised Clete, it was nothing compared to how I astounded myself. Clete backed slowly out of the yard and rushed off down the street, and I wondered why the hurry until I realized that the gun wasn't in its holster anymore, it was in my hand, and my hand was trembling, and not from the cold.

Clete stayed away, but he sent me a message nearly every day from then on, by the Doc when he came to see Pap or Becky Lynn, or by Mr. Floyd when he delivered an order, or by boys I knew who just happened to stop by. Clete figured Becky Lynn was his now. He meant to have her, even if it meant going through me to get her, and he hoped it did. I never let on to Mrs. Johnson about Clete's threats. The rest of the town could hold their breaths if they had a mind to. Clete knew where to find me, and I had better things to do than wait around to see if he meant to do me harm.

Valentine's Day was coming along fast, and I decided to go ahead and get Becky Lynn that engagement ring out of the money Doc gave Pap and me for the farm. There would still be plenty left to pay our rent for months to come, and next summer I'd find a place for me and Becky Lynn to farm on our own, so we could always be together and I wouldn't have to worry anymore. I hadn't decided what to do about Pap when that time came, and I didn't want to leave Mrs. Johnson to take care of him all by herself. After all, she was already nursemaid and cook, and she was only supposed to be renting him a room. For that matter, I didn't want to leave Mrs. Johnson. Maybe, when I found a suitable piece of land, we could all move there as a family.

It was raining the evening of February fourteenth, a cold, freezing rain. Becky Lynn had been in the kitchen most of the afternoon, and I knew she and Mrs. Johnson were cooking up a special supper, and it sure did smell good. I was so glad to see Becky Lynn in motion, participating in life again. I puttered around the house most of the day and visited with Pap in his room and talked his ear off about marrying Becky Lynn. I even told him I was going to buy her a ring, knowing that he wouldn't respond and wouldn't reveal my secret.

There was a good fire going in the fireplace that afternoon, and the house fit my idea of what Heaven would have to be like, a warm place where you knew you belonged with people who loved you so much it almost hurt. I told Mrs. Johnson and Becky Lynn I was going to take a short walk and would be back within an hour or so. It was the first time I had left them alone since I quit working at the general store, but the nasty weather should keep company away, and I didn't figure on being gone very long. I bundled up and wore gloves and a wool scarf, but it was still plenty cold, and I had to walk real careful to keep from slipping on the ice that was forming all over the place.

As I had hoped, the mercantile was empty. I went in and talked to stone-faced old Mrs. Shanks and told her I wanted to buy a ring with a diamond in it. The way she looked at me, she must've thought I was the devil's own issue, because she knew who I was buying it for, and all the good people in town knew that girl should've already been handed over to her rightful suitor by now, instead of committing a blatant sin and marrying a different man than the one who'd claimed her. I smiled at poor old Mrs. Shanks and wondered at the years of injustice that had marred her face with gullies and crevasses of hopelessness and despair.

I laid the bills in her stiff, bony hand and she handed me a little box with the ring inside, wrapped in a shiny piece of white satin. It reminded me of Mama's watch box. The freezing rain had turned into hard little balls of sleet by the time I stepped outside. Mrs. Shanks locked the door behind me. Farther down the street,

Mr. Floyd was locking up the general store. He paused for a look at me and hurried away without returning my wave.

I took my time walking home, going over in my mind all the different ways I could come up with to give Becky Lynn her ring. I couldn't wait to see the look on her face. The ring would convince her once and for all that I really and truly meant to marry her. And I would love her, really love her, so gentle and sweet and slow that she would forget the hell she had gone through at the hands of Clete Parker. At least I hoped so. I might not be her very first, but I wanted to be her best and her only, and I knew I could treat her right.

I smelled smoke before I turned off the last block toward home. Of course everybody was burning wood in fireplaces and stoves, but this smelled heavier somehow, thick enough to taste, and then I heard horses screeching and people yelling, and I ran the rest of the way to the corner, expecting to see our neighbor's barn on fire.

Flames shot skyward through the roof of the boarding house, and people stopped me from charging inside when I got there. I kept yelling that my Pap was in there, and where was Becky Lynn and her mama, until I found Mrs. Johnson sprawled in the snow against the shed watching her world turn to ashes. There was a horrified look on her face, and I realized she wasn't seeing the fire.

Where's Pap, I yelled, shaking her by the shoulders, did they get Pap out of there! She shook her head and said he went back inside. I thought she had lost her mind, and then she squeezed my hand and looked up at me and said that Becky Lynn was gone. I thought she meant Becky Lynn was still in that burning house, and I turned to run, but she held onto my hand and shook her head and cried without tears, as though there weren't any left to wash away her grief.

I pulled away from Mrs. Johnson and tried to find a way inside the house, but it was burning everywhere at once. I yelled for Pap until I was hoarse and kept looking for somebody who might've seen Becky Lynn come out, but nobody could tell me anything about either of them.

The neighbors, Mr. and Mrs. Wakefield, came and got Mrs. Johnson and took her to their house, but she refused to go unless I came, too, so I went along just to get her settled in and then I was going to go back and look for Doc. He might have gotten Pap out of that house, might have taken Pap down to his office here in town. And I wanted Mrs. Johnson to tell me where I could find Becky Lynn.

Mr. and Mrs. Wakefield set Mrs. Johnson down on a feather mattress in their oldest daughter's bedroom and left us alone. Mrs. Johnson pulled me down beside her and gasped out the story no one else wanted to hear.

Clete came for Becky Lynn while I was away. He kicked the front door in and demanded his bride. When Becky Lynn hid, Clete threw his bottle of liquor at the fireplace, and when it broke and poured across the floor, the house caught fire. Desperate to get away, Becky Lynn ran out the back door and into the woods. Mrs. Johnson tried to follow, but Clete hit her over the head with a skillet and left her unconscious on the kitchen floor.

She woke up in the snow beside the shed. And as I stood in that same spot and watched my home burn to the ground, I visualized what Mrs. Johnson must have seen when she regained consciousness, as my eyes followed two narrow wheel tracks all the way back to the ramp by the kitchen door.

Tears came then, and I remember thinking I must've cried more in the past seven months than in all my life before. Pap was dead, though he'd found the strength, physically and emotionally, to save someone else's life before choosing his own fate. It was his only chance to die a hero, and he took advantage of the opportunity. In a strange, sad way, I understood and respected his decision, and I hoped he was shaking hands with the good Lord he used to mention now and then.

Mrs. Johnson was homeless, and Becky Lynn – oh, if she hadn't escaped, what Clete would've done to Becky Lynn! It was so cold out, and she had left without a coat, so even if she found a place to hide, she wouldn't be safe.

I found the sheriff and told him what happened, but he didn't seem interested in looking for Becky Lynn. Clete'll bring her back, he said. I followed their prints on the slushy ground until they disappeared into the darkness of the woods. It was a black night, too dark to see. I went to the Wakefields' house and sat in their kitchen until the first light, and then I picked up the trail in the woods and followed the path Becky Lynn and I always took when we walked together, past our sweetheart tree, through the meadow where we watched the deer, along the bluff above the creek bed.

I found Becky Lynn crumpled in the tall brown reeds beside the pond. Her skirt was up over her head, and I pulled it down past her knees without looking at her naked midsection. The top of her dress had been ripped open, and frozen blood was crusted around the bite marks along the tops of her breasts. Vicious bruises encircled her slender neck where brutal hands had stopped the flow of blood, air, and life.

Her eyes were wide and staring, her hair frozen to the ground. I couldn't even gather her up into my arms to hold her. I knelt over her and smothered her face in kisses and wept for the loss of my wife, my father, my home.

The sheriff was at the boarding house when I got back, looking through the rubble with a few other men. Mrs. Johnson waited there, too, and she ran right to me and asked if I'd seen any sign of Becky Lynn. I just looked at her, and I guess she must've figured it out, because she burst into tears, and Mrs. Wakefield came running over to hug her and lead her back to the house next door.

I walked up to the sheriff and told him Becky Lynn Johnson had been strangled to death by Clete Parker the night before. I told him Clete had tried to kill Mrs. Johnson as well, had burned down their house, and was responsible for my Pap's death in the fire. I told him Becky Lynn's raped and tortured body lay frozen to the ground on this side of Shoffner's pond.

The sheriff said I had a lot of nerve, accusing Clete Parker of all those terrible things. He asked me where I got that fancy word and what it meant, and I told him I read about it in a newspaper the doctor brought from Statler Ridge, that it was a punishable crime up there to force yourself on an unwilling young woman. The sheriff said he'd never heard of Becky Lynn being unwilling, and I hauled off and busted his mouth with my fist. His first inclination was to arrest me right then and there, but he just held a handkerchief to his bleeding lip and told the men to let go of me, I'd been under a lot of pressure losing my Pap and all, and now Becky Lynn must've gone off and killed herself, so it was natural that I would to want to lash out at someone. He told me to go somewhere and cool off and get all those ridiculous notions out of my head, because he wouldn't be so forgiving if I tried to pick a fight again.

I told him the only thing ridiculous was that Clete had not been held responsible for forcing himself on Becky Lynn in the first place. The sheriff told me to cool off again, said he and the doctor both went and talked with Clete after that little incident, and Clete explained that he had Becky Lynn's consent to get intimate with her. And besides, she didn't look near as bad as she made out to be that evening.

There must have been some kind of look on my face, 'cause the sheriff actually took a step backwards and two men moved up to take hold of my arms again. I didn't yell or go crazy or kill anybody, like I truly felt it necessary to do. I just told the sheriff that those were the charges, and me and Mrs. Johnson were bringing them up against Clete Parker, and he could prepare to defend himself as soon as Judge Reed was ready.

The sheriff acted all mad, but he was still careful to keep some distance between us, and he said he'd send some men down to Shoffner's pond to pick up Becky Lynn. He said he'd pass the word along to Judge Reed if I was sure I felt the need to stir everybody up over nothing. Then he walked away quick, glancing back at me until he got out to the street, though I hadn't said another word, but maybe my expression gave away what I was thinking.

Becky Lynn was buried three days later. Her wake was held at the church, since Mrs. Johnson didn't have a home anymore. People brought food to the Wakefields' house, where Mrs.

Johnson was staying.

Right after her funeral there was a short memorial service for Pap, though we didn't have much to bury, just a sealed box of charred remains that Doc said I'd best not see. People stood around uncomfortable while Doc said a few nice things, because none of them knew Pap and most had never even met him. They just looked at me like they didn't understand how I could've lost what they never knew I had to begin with.

Becky Lynn was laid to rest beside her Papa, with a space between them that Mrs. Johnson would occupy someday. The ground was frozen solid on the surface, and I wondered how old Mr. Sheppard ever got the grave dug, and I worried that Becky Lynn would be cold and scared down there alone in the dark.

Mr. Floyd let me sleep in the general store next to the wood stove. For a week after Becky Lynn's funeral, I'd get up every morning and walk to the Wakefields' house and sit across the table from Mrs. Johnson and we would stare at each other like we was each begging the other to please wake us both up from this awful dream. The only thing we talked about, all that was on both our minds, was seeing Clete Parker pay for what he had done.

Judge Reed agreed to hold an informal hearing ten days after Becky Lynn was buried. The little church that served as a school house also served as a court house, and every man in town turned out that day to see what me and Mrs. Johnson might have to say against Clete Parker and how Judge Reed was gonna go about closing the situation.

I noticed right off there were no women in the room. Not one.

The sheriff took Mrs. Johnson by the arm and led her all the way up front and sat her down in a chair right in front of the pulpit. I was following them, but Mr. Shanks stood up so quick I almost ran into him. He pointed to a chair in the second row next to Mr. Floyd. I took my seat, figuring they were going to let Mrs. Johnson go first, and when she got through, I would have my turn defending Becky Lynn and Pap in that unfriendly little straight-backed chair.

Judge Reed arrived and clomped up front and sat down on the

long low bench that served as an altar on Sundays and a step stool the rest of the week for children too short to reach the blackboard. I waited for him to remove his hat, but he didn't, and I knew he wasn't going to take me and Mrs. Johnson seriously, and I started getting mad. Judge Reed only removed his hat for trials and funerals, and he apparently didn't afford this episode the importance of either one.

The only person who hadn't bothered to show up yet was Clete Parker. He swaggered in twenty minutes beyond the appointed time, slapping buddies on the back as if he were making a routine stop by the general store. Clete's pap strolled along behind him with his thumbs hooked in his suspenders and his chest stuck out, proud as a bantam rooster. Mr. Parker wheezed like water bubbling through a straw, and that day his asthmatic complications somehow emphasized his arrogant pride in the infamy his son was being accorded.

Clete leered at Mrs. Johnson as he strolled past, fixing his eyes greedily on her chest. He glanced back at his audience and waggled his eyebrows, earning howls of laughter as Mrs. Johnson turned beet red and tears formed in the corners of her eyes. From where I sat, I could see her profile, and I started to stand up in her defense, but Mr. Floyd grabbed my arm and pulled me back down. Somebody else clapped a hand on my shoulder from behind. I knew then that this trial was nothing more than a big joke, but I severely underestimated Clete's performance.

Judge Reed just sat there looking bored. When the laughter died down, he studied his watch with an exaggerated frown and looked up at Clete with, "I'm glad you could see fit to join us, son," and everybody laughed again.

Judge Reed waited until the room got quiet, and then he motioned toward Clete. "You know what the charges are, son." He directed a disparaging look toward Mrs. Johnson. She was visibly trembling, clenching and unclenching her fists, staring straight ahead at the blackboard as a tear slowly crept down the side of her face. "What have you got to say about it?"

Clete turned to face Mrs. Johnson. He was a giant, and as he loomed over Mrs. Johnson sitting in that chair, she seemed to shrink even smaller from the meanness in those piggish eyes. She glanced up at his face and resumed staring at the blackboard.

"I really don't know what all the fuss is about, Judge." Clete shrugged with helpless abandon. He smiled around the room as if embarrassed. "We all know the disposition of an innkeeper's daughter." He paced back and forth in front of Mrs. Johnson, looking her over, degrading her with his lingering gazes at the front of her dress. "Mrs. Johnson, I know you'd like to think Becky Lynn was just a sweet, innocent girl, but truth is, she was all woman when she was with me. She liked it hard and fast, and I daresay she must've picked up some experience somewhere along the way." He smirked at me, where I was held in my seat by Mr. Floyd and the men behind us. Then he stopped right in front of Mrs. Johnson, so close he was practically standing on her toes, and grinned sloppily down at the top of her head. "I could give you the details if you'd like to hear them," he taunted, "of where your little girl put her hands on me, and what she begged me to do to her when she discovered the extent of my equipment—"

Something along the lines of a roar burst from Mrs. Johnson's throat and she shot up from that chair and shoved Clete backward so hard that he landed on Judge Reed's altar seat a split second after Judge Reed saw him coming and moved out of the way.

That roomful of men was so surprised that nobody said a word. Clete stood up uncertainly, like he wasn't sure what hit him, and Judge Reed stood still and stared at Mrs. Johnson's face, red with anger and wet with tears, until he remembered his position in this crucial confrontation.

"That will be quite enough, Mrs. Johnson!" the judge boomed out. "Take your seat and let Clete finish. And Clete..." Judge Reed shooed him out of the way so he could sit back down. "Don't get so close to Mrs. Johnson from here on out, in case she loses control again."

Clete backed away from Mrs. Johnson with exaggerated caution, looking around the room, meeting men's eyes to drive home the point that, as you can all see, this woman is crazy!

Then his attitude changed. He was tired of playing and was ready to end the game. Clete walked back over to Mrs. Johnson and looked down at her as though viewing something unspeakably disgusting. He directed that same expression at Judge Reed as though he didn't matter, either. "The point is—" Clete stood tall and turned to his audience "—everything I did, I did *with Becky Lynn's consent.* She knew what was going to happen, she wanted it to happen, she encouraged it to happen, and when her boyfriend got upset, she changed her story and said I forced her. She lied to her mama, and she lied to him." Clete looked down his nose at me, an unworthy opponent. "Last week Becky Lynn sent word that she wanted to see me. I went over to the house, and Becky Lynn and I went for a walk. While we were out the boarding house caught fire. I saw it from Shoffner's pond and ran back to see if I could help put it out. I'm afraid in my haste I left Becky Lynn behind. She'd been talking about marriage, you know, and I had to tell her I just wasn't ready for that kind of thing. I guess she got upset and killed herself after I left her up there."

That was my breaking point. I jumped to my feet, shaking off Mr. Floyd and lunging free of the men who held me from behind. *"You murdered her!"* I screamed. "You raped her and you murdered her because that's the only way you would ever have her at all! Becky Lynn Johnson hated the very sight of you! The very thought of being alone with you made her sick! She was in love with me, she was going to marry me, so *you murdered her!"* I yelled the last as I was hurled out the door into the mud and slush by Mr. Shanks and Mr. Floyd and Clete's younger brother, Clyde, who saw fit to knuckle punch me in the groin as they threw me out the door. I knew I wasn't going to get back inside, so I staggered around the church until I came to a window across from where Mrs. Johnson was sitting. I pried it up a couple of inches so I could hear what was going on. I'd go through the glass, if I had to, before I'd let them lay a hand on Mrs. Johnson.

Clete was smirking. The victory had been his all along, but it was sweet nonetheless. All he had to do was finish off the opposition. He walked right up to Mrs. Johnson and looked down at her once more. "What you're not telling everybody," he informed her, "is that Becky Lynn and I asked your permission to go for a walk in the woods because it was kind of late and we weren't sure if it would be all right with you if we went out. And you said it was all right, Mrs. Johnson. You gave both of us your permission to go out together."

"I never did that!" Mrs. Johnson cried out, but something in Clete's eyes cut off anything else she might have said. He leaned forward, putting a hand on each arm of the straight wood chair, surrounding Mrs. Johnson with his vile presence. She lost the reassurance of the blackboard, staring into that huge face, just inches from her own. She resembled nothing so much as a tiny bird looking up to find itself between the front paws of a wolf and knowing with helpless certainty that it was over – with a pathetic attempt at resistance and with desperate panic and finally with bitter resignation, that it was over.

"If you don't remember, Mrs. Johnson, just say so." Clete's voice was low and menacing. "I won't be upset if you don't remember. But don't say it didn't happen. Don't say you didn't give me and Becky Lynn permission to be together. Because you did. *You did.* Just say you don't remember."

He waited, not moving, breathing in Mrs. Johnson's face. She was being threatened and she knew it and there was nothing she could do about it. Every man in the room was waiting for her to confirm Clete's story. Every man in the room knew that she would.

"Well, Mrs. Johnson?" Clete put his left hand under her chin and yanked her face up to his. "I didn't hear your answer. Do you remember, or don't you?"

"No," Mrs. Johnson whispered.

"No, what, Mrs. Johnson, I don't think anybody else heard you!" Clete held onto her face with his left hand and deliberately curled his right into a clenched fist.

"I don't remember!" Mrs. Johnson sobbed. She jerked away from Clete and bent over in the chair, hiding her face with her hands, her body shaking violently with the overflow of grief and rage and injustice.

"There you have it." Clete loomed over his prey. "Not only did I have Becky Lynn's consent, I also had her mother's consent!" He turned toward the altar with a grin. "Anything else, Judge?"

"What about it, Mrs. Johnson?" Judge Reed demanded. "If you don't have anything else to complain about, can we all go home now?"

Mrs. Johnson leaned forward with her face in her hands, sobbing hysterically. The men slapped each other on the back as they filed out the door celebrating another uprising brought down. Women just don't know their place, proclaimed one. Well, what else are they good for, brayed another. She could've fought him off and walked away! That was Clyde, the rapist's brother. I wondered why someone as small as Becky Lynn was assumed to be strong enough to fight off something the size of Clete Parker, when on the other hand women were too weak and stupid to even make their own decisions.

When the last of them had snorted, burped, and wheezed away, I went in and got Mrs. Johnson and took her to the Wakefields' house. Mr. Wakefield had not gone to the trial. He had too much respect for Mrs. Walkefield to participate in such a farce.

Mrs. Wakefield made Mrs. Johnson lie down and get some rest. I sat at the kitchen table and guzzled hot black coffee and loaded and unloaded Pap's pistol. I had nothing to lose now. I was making plans when Mrs. Wakefield told me I had a visitor.

Doc stood on the front porch holding Pap's shotgun and a pouch full of shells. "Thought you might like to have this back, seeing as how you lost everything else in the fire."

It was decent of him to think like that, and I told him so, but I remembered him laughing at Clete Parker's jokes that morning while Mrs. Johnson cried, so I didn't hang around on the porch to talk to him. I went back into the kitchen and cleaned Pap's shotgun and slid a shell into the chamber. Then, hating myself for what I was fast becoming, hating that there was no other way justice would ever be served, I propped the shotgun in the corner beside Mrs. Wakefield's cupboard and hung my holster on a hook by the door. I put on my jacket and went for one last walk as a free man.

I should have known I couldn't have been the only one thinking to avenge Becky Lynn and Pap and Mrs. Johnson.

Mrs. Wakefield's sewing was interrupted by a loud noise in the kitchen. When she walked in she saw a cloth bag of shells spilling across the table. Pap's shotgun was gone.

And so was Mrs. Johnson.

Mrs. Johnson walked out of town carrying Pap's shotgun and took the path to the Parker place. Clete lived with his Pap and two younger brothers, a houseful of oversized men.

Mrs. Johnson walked in to find them sitting down to dinner. Mr. Parker backed away from the stove when she came through the door, wheezing at the sight of her. Clete stood and came around the table, smiling with his most affable charm, approaching her with the same soft, soothing voice he used to catch kittens and puppies in order to tie them up in a feed sack and drown them in the pond. Clyde and Clem just sat there, staring dumbly over their stew.

Mrs. Johnson raised the shotgun, stopping Clete in his tracks. Clete sweet-talked her, complimented her, sympathized with her, understood everything about her, as he tried to get close enough to grab the gun away. Mr. Parker panted closer and had the audacity to beg her not to kill his oldest son, his pride and joy, so dear to his heart. Mrs. Johnson looked Mr. Parker in the eye.

And she smiled.

"It's all right," she told him. "I have Becky Lynn's consent."

Mrs. Johnson raised the barrel to Clete Parker's belt and pulled the trigger. The blast blew him near in two. As he fell back against the table and collapsed to the floor, she reached into the pocket of her apron and retrieved a second shell. She levered it into the chamber, pushed the barrel of the shotgun against Clete's face, and pulled the trigger again. Clete's head disappeared in a red spray that painted the wall behind him and spattered everyone in the room.

She loaded the gun a third time as Mr. Parker's wheezes progressed to agonized sputters. She turned the gun on him, but didn't have to use it. With a hand over his heart and pain etched deep into his purple face, Mr. Parker sank to the floor struggling for air, and Mrs. Johnson watched him suffocate.

"My son," he gasped.

"Died," Mrs. Johnson assured him, "with Becky Lynn's consent."

That's the story twelve-year-old Clem Parker told the whole town. Mrs. Johnson walked out, he said, as soon as she heard Mr. Parker's last breath escape in one long, gurgling rush.

Mrs. Johnson returned to the Wakefields' house and propped the shotgun against the cupboard where she had found it. She took Pap's pistol, my pistol, out of the holster I had left hanging by the door. She walked next door to her own property and sat on the woodpile behind the home she had shared with her in-laws, her husband, her daughter. She looked at everything that was no longer there. She raised the pistol to her head, Mrs. Wakefield screamed from the kitchen window, and Mrs. Johnson took her own life.

Mr. Wakefield met me in the back yard when I returned from Shoffner's pond, and he told me that Mrs. Johnson had enforced justice on behalf of Becky Lynn and my Pap. I had been gone just long enough for Clem Parker to run to town and spread the news. Cassius Parker and Clete were dead. Clyde was in a stupor and wouldn't talk to anybody. Clem had lost control of his bladder and his sanity and no one could calm him down.

None of that mattered to me. I pulled the sheet back from Mrs. Johnson's body and held her in my arms, weeping for my mama and for my long lost baby sister and for Pap and the misdirected logic that kept him from ever truly giving or receiving love.

Mrs. Johnson looked perfect except for the small hole in her right temple. Her features were relaxed and she was pretty again, like when Pap and me first moved to town. I kissed her face and covered her back up. I went to the general store and filled a knapsack with food and matches and a pair of socks and left without paying for any of it. Nobody tried to stop me.

I hitchhiked to Statler Ridge, where I slipped into an empty boxcar and rode northwest to Illinois. I stepped out in a city bigger than I could have ever imagined and got a job in a factory and an apartment no bigger than Mrs. Johnson's parlor.

I learned about the opposite extreme there. I saw meek little men striving to please domineering brides. I met women who were quite open about their sexuality. Some were downright brazen and expected money in return for their time and attention. Women educated themselves, held jobs, earned money, owned property, and if they weren't treated as equals, they were at least left alone.

I joined the army and got to travel to some of the places I had read about in Mrs. Johnson's books. I made friends, learned how to get along without getting lost, and managed to grow up before I grew old. Most important of all, I never forgot where I came from.

Through the years I met a couple of genuine ladies, beautiful and gracious, who would have made better brides than a man should have the right to ask for. But each wanted something that wasn't mine to give, 'cause my heart is buried with Becky Lynn back yonder by Hazel Creek. I've lived alone, and lived with regrets, lots of them, though I don't rightly know what I could've done that would've changed the outcome of anything.

But some nights, when I am feeling forlorn and waiting for the call Pap strained so hard to hear, I take a little box out of my bureau and unfold the yellowed square of satin inside and study the diamond, clear as water, perched atop a shining golden halo. If I concentrate very hard, I can hear Becky Lynn's voice calling through the years, the melody of her laughter, the love in my name on her lips.

Somewhere there is innocence, a Heaven where virtue is protected and cherished and nurtured until it grows into knowledge and maturity without compromising compassion and truth. That's where I'll find Becky Lynn, waiting for the day when we will be reunited in a place where life is perfect, and love means everything, and happiness is a promise that won't ever go away.

Once Upon A Weekend

Katy leaned across the back of the sofa and peered out the window into the dusk. There was more to hear than to see; the big man across the street was yelling at his woman again, his tirade disturbingly out of place in the serene suburban neighborhood.

Katy continued to observe the house across the street as darkness closed in and voices fell silent. Lights came on in surrounding homes, and televisions flickered to life beyond thinly veiled windows. Children abandoned toys in dew-damp grass and went inside for the evening. A quiet peace enveloped Katy's little corner of the world, just like 'most every night for as long as she could remember.

The big man yelled again. Katy wondered if other people could hear him, and if they could, why they didn't make him stop. His woman was frail and timid. She had reached out to Katy on the sidewalk once, and the big man had yelled at her for that, too. What could she possibly do, Katy wondered, to deserve such cruel treatment every day.

Eventually the sitter lifted her hefty frame from the armchair and nudged Katy aside to close the window. Katy accompanied Miss May to the kitchen for supper. By the time Katy returned to her spot on the sofa, night had overtaken the earth, leaving the neighborhood completely, mercifully, silent.

Just as Katy turned to join Miss May in front of the television, she detected movement across the street. A large shadow glided among the others along the carport. With a glint of metal and a covert glance, the shadow slunk out of sight behind the house.

It was more than Katy's curiosity could stand. She looked at the sitter, heavily involved in prime time drama. If Katy was careful, Miss May would never know she had gone.

Katy slipped off the sofa and padded quietly behind the sitter's chair through the dining room to the kitchen. After listening for a moment – Miss May's attention was still riveted on the movie – Katy stole out the back door.

Staying close to the shrubbery, Katy trotted around the house, paused to look both ways, and shot across the dim street. She hesitated beside a tree in the big man's front yard, spooked when a cricket chirped, and almost fled back to the safety of her own living room. But she had come this far. Just a quick look to see who was doing what behind the house, and she would leave as quietly as she had arrived, and no one would ever know she had been here at all.

Katy took a deep breath and mustered the courage to approach the carport. She gave the big man's truck plenty of room. It reeked of his cigars. The scent made Katy nauseous. Beyond the carport a sparse hedge of unkempt rose bushes extended along the driveway to the far end of the back yard, offering sufficient cover in the dark. Katy crept along the border until she spotted a gap large enough to wriggle through. She went no farther.

The big man stood with his back to her. Her eyes had not deceived her. He wielded a shovel, ripping great chunks out of the soft earth, piling dirt and sod into a wheelbarrow. The woman had tilled the garden three days past in preparation for planting. What did the big man intend to plant that required such a big, deep hole, and why was he digging against the grape arbor? Nothing would grow there; a mantle of grapevines would drape that whole area in a few weeks. Even Katy knew that.

Katy shrank back against the rose hedge and knelt to watch. Though terrified of being caught, she had seen too much to leave now. She waited while the big man dug for an hour more. Katy grew restless. Bedtime was approaching. Miss May would be looking for her and would be quite unhappy if she discovered that Katy had gone outside after dark.

The big man finally stepped out of the hole and threw the shovel to the ground. He disappeared inside the unlit house and stumbled out the door moments later under the weight of a rolled tarp. He carried his burden to the hole, shifted it in his arms, and –

Katy gasped and turned to run, forgetting the thorny hedge. She was instantly entangled and discovered. As the big man turned and stared into her face, Katy began thrashing about in terror.

"You!" He flung the tarp into the hole, picked up the shovel, and walked slowly and deliberately toward Katy. "I've warned you about sneaking around here. I've told you to stay off my property. Well, it's time you learned a lesson, you little brat! I'm going to enjoy this." He grinned maliciously.

As he raised the shovel, Katy gave one last lunge and wrenched free of the thorns. She fled past the carport, across the street, and through the back door of her own house, not caring how much noise she made. She ran to the living room where world news now blared from the television screen, and turned to the sitter with wide, terrified eyes.

Miss May lounged motionless with her head tilted back, snoring softly. Katy arranged herself beside the armchair, as close to the sitter as she could get, and trembled as she listened for the big man to come after her.

Though Mom and Dad stood by the rule that Katy sleep in her own bed, the sitter saw no reason to be so strict. Katy slept with Miss May in the guest room and kept one eye and one ear on duty all night.

The next morning Katy was still upset. She picked at her breakfast, causing Miss May to question if she felt ill. Katy did feel ill, but not physically. The very real nightmare she had experienced left her jumpy and afraid. It also left her with a very uncomfortable responsibility. Katy knew she needed to tell someone what she had seen, but she did not know how to go about it. She thought at last of someone she could tell, but cringed at the thought of talking to *him*.

After breakfast Miss May occupied herself with light housework. Katy went out the back door and cut across two adjoining yards before stopping several feet from a chain link fence. Tony was out, as she knew he would be, playing roughly with a variety of toys. Katy always felt intimidated in his presence. Though a year younger, Tony stood much taller and far more powerfully built than Katy. He was deliberately unfriendly and made it a point to mistreat Katy verbally whenever he saw her, because he could not run fast enough to catch her. Katy approached the yard reluctantly, thankful for the fence between them.

Tony's observational skills were, Katy thought as she shook her head, incredibly dull. Minutes dragged by, and still he remained oblivious to her presence. She finally cleared her throat to get his attention.

Tony froze, cocked his head, and scanned the fence row until his eyes fell on Katy. He glared at her with contempt and turned back to his toys as though she were not even there.

"Tony," Katy began. She paused, pulled herself up tall, and started over.

"Tony, I..." she really did *hate* to ask him. "I need some advice."

Tony shrugged and tossed aside a mangled plastic car stolen from a neighborhood boy. "Go chase yourself," he offered.

Katy lowered her eyes and prayed for patience. She tried again. "It's important, Tony. Something terrible has happened, and I need your help."

"Hey, I don't want my friends to see me talking to the likes of you," Tony said. "They might get the wrong idea or something. You could ruin my reputation just by being here, so why don't you get lost!"

"Well, I don't want my friends to see me associating with you, either!" Katy retorted. Then, remembering the situation, she relented. "Okay, have it your way." She crouched and shouldered her way between the chain link barrier on her left and the weeds and vines that grew along the fence row to her right, until she couldn't be seen except by Tony from inside his yard. "*Now* will you listen to me?"

"If it's that important, tell your mom and dad," Tony said to a warped Frisbee.

"They're not home," Katy said. "They went away for the weekend. A sitter is staying at my house until they get back."

"So, tell the sitter."

"She wouldn't believe me. Mom told her I have an overactive imagination and warned her to believe about half of what I say, and that only after she has verified the story for herself. Tony, this is an emergency!"

"Can't you dial 911?"

"I'm not allowed to use the phone." Katy examined her nails, embarrassed. "I tried to call someone a long time ago, but I didn't know how. I had seen Mom pushing the buttons, so I pushed them all, but no one ever talked to me. I forgot to put the receiver back in place, and Mom got really upset about that. She told the sitter to not let me near the phone."

Tony examined a worn baseball and pretended to ignore Katy, but she did not go away. She sat and stared at him until he thought he would explode. At length, he did. "Look, I'm not interested in your problems! Go away and leave me alone! Get away from my yard!" He stood and stepped menacingly toward Katy.

Katy knew she was safe behind the fence. And she finally had his attention.

"The big man across the street murdered his wife last night," Katy said casually.

Tony was aware of Katy's flair for the dramatic, but this was extreme, even for her. He stopped and studied her face. Katy stared back, without blinking, until he had to look away. It drove him crazy and made him hate her.

"What makes you think he murdered her?" Tony asked, giving a little. "The big man always yells and throws things, even at us. He's mean to everybody, but he's never killed anyone that we know of."

"He killed Thomas."

"Thomas got hit by a car."

"Thomas was run over by a truck. *His* truck." Katy looked bitterly toward the big man's house. "And last night he killed his wife."

"How?"

"I don't know how. I didn't see that part. But I saw him bury her in his back yard."

"You shouldn't go into his back yard. And just because he buried something doesn't mean it was his *wife*, for Pete's sake."

"It was his wife. I saw her arm."

Tony looked at her skeptically.

"It was his wife," Katy insisted. "He wrapped her in a tarp, and her arm dangled out of it before he put her in the hole he had dug. I saw the whole thing."

Tony sat down and took a deep breath while the news sank in. Then he shrugged carelessly at Katy.

"So why tell me? Even if the big man did murder his wife, there's nothing I can do about it!"

"You can dig her up," Katy suggested.

Tony looked at Katy like she had lost her mind as he searched for an excuse.

"Mom and Dad won't let me out of the yard," he said.

"Oh, please!" Katy was tired of being patient. "You come out any time you darn well please when you want to give *me* grief! You find it easy enough to leave your yard when you want to bully the neighborhood children or terrify their pets. The fence hasn't stopped you yet."

Wheedling and goading had never been Katy's style, but she had seen Tony employ such tactics on many occasions and knew what his reaction would be. Smiling craftily, she stood to leave. "Of course, if you're scared, I certainly understand," she said as she turned away.

"Scared!" Tony huffed, and rose to follow Katy along the other side of the fence. "I am *not* scared! People are scared of *me*! You know that!"

"Oh, yeah," Katy sauntered to the end of the yard and headed back toward her own house. "Sure, Tony. Whatever you say."

"Wait! Katy…come back," Tony growled from the corner of the fence, looking around to make sure no one saw him talking to her.

Katy smiled to herself, returned to the fence, and sat down facing Tony.

"What, then?" she blinked innocently.

"Well…" Tony sighed and sat down, too. "*If* the big man murdered his wife, we have to let someone know."

"Your mom and dad?" Katy suggested.

Tony shook his head. "My mom and dad are like yours. They wouldn't believe me if I tried to tell them something like that. And I lost my phone privileges, too." He didn't bother to tell her how. "Do you have any ideas?"

"You could dig her up," Katy said for the second time. "Tonight, if you can get away. It's no trouble for me to slip out. My sitter could sleep through the Second Coming. I can be the lookout while you dig."

"If digging's all there is to do, why don't you just do it?" snapped Tony, remembering who was making the suggestion.

"Because you're a lot bigger than me and you can do it a lot faster," Katy said, swallowing her frustration. "And I don't know who else to ask. But you're right. There is more to it than that. After we uncover her, we have to get someone to come into the big man's back yard and find her, and nobody *ever* goes there. That part won't be easy, but I'll figure something out by tonight. Will you help me?"

Tony grunted. Katy had been an enemy for as long as he could remember, and he enjoyed maintaining that relationship. But if something terrible happened in their neighborhood, shouldn't they all take part in making things right? He made himself look at Katy and tried to conceal his disdain for the impertinent little scamp.

"Okay," he said through clenched teeth. "I'll help. But you had better be telling me the truth, or I will bury *you* in the big man's back yard!"

Katy smiled the superior smile Tony hated. "Come to my front yard after the late movie is over," she instructed. "We'll go across the street together, and I will show you where the big man buried his wife."

She trotted away, pleased at her success and weak with relief that the confrontation was over.

Tony watched her go, wishing he never had to see her again.

Late that afternoon Katy sat in Miss May's lap, digesting a midday snack and getting sleepy while the sitter gently combed her hair. Brilliant rays of sun reached through the venetian blinds and painted inviting stripes of warmth across the carpet. Katy watched dust particles dance in the light until a shadow eclipsed the room. She flinched and looked toward the window, half expecting to see the big man from across the street. What she did see wasn't much better. She excused herself from the sitter and walked out into the back yard.

Tony was still peering through the window when she came around the side of the house. Katy sat on the grass a few feet behind him and contemplated all the ways she could have fun with this situation. However, exposing the big man and his crime took priority over the brief thrill of momentary vengeance, and it required cooperation on both her and Tony's part.

A brief look around verified escape routes and places to hide in case Tony reacted in keeping with his usual self. Katy softly spoke his name.

Tony whirled around, tripping over his own feet. "If you ever scare me like that again, I'll bite you clean in two."

"Why are you here?" Katy gracefully ignored the threat.

"I started thinking," Tony began, and Katy had to hold her

breath to contain the sarcastic remarks that begged release. "If we could go to the big man's yard while it's still daylight and dig the woman up, maybe you or I could get one of the neighbors to chase us through the yard and find her."

Katy knew of several reasons that would not work. "She's buried at the far end of the garden, but in plain view of the house, and it's Saturday, so the big man didn't go to work today. He would surely see us. Even if he didn't, we'd never get one of the neighbors to chase us through his back yard. They sacrifice their kid's toys that fall over his hedge rather than set foot on his property."

Tony grunted with disappointment, but he knew Katy was right.

"But if we can't draw attention to the dead woman now, how are we going to do it after dark?"

"I'll take care of that," Katy said, wishing she really did have a plan.

Tony was perplexed, but didn't want to sound too interested in anything Katy had to say. He lifted his nose just high enough to look down it at her.

"I'll see you tonight, then," he said, and headed off toward a neighbor's flower bed.

Katy played outside alone for the rest of the afternoon. She ate a light supper, washed up, and watched the sun set from her usual window. She played games with the sitter and napped during prime time. When Miss May dozed off during the late movie, Katy quietly let herself out the back door and waited for Tony behind the shrubs.

No conversation passed between them when he arrived at two a.m. Katy led the way across the street, past the big man's carport, and to the rose hedge without stopping. Tony leaped over the hedge while Katy crawled under. They waited until they were positive no one else was in the yard, and then Katy broke the silence.

"Over there at the garden's edge. By the grape arbor, practically beneath it."

"The whole strip looks like garden to me."

"Of course it does. Last night he put the excess dirt in a wheelbarrow so the ground wouldn't be mounded up where he buried the woman."

"Well." Tony looked warily at the dark house "Let's go."

"Wait." Katy actually touched him. "There aren't many places to hide around here, and you're a lot bigger than me. If the big man comes out, I can climb a tree or make for the undergrowth beyond the grape arbor. But where will you hide?"

"I won't have to hide," Tony said haughtily. "He'd have to be out of his mind to come after me."

Katy shuddered. She was truly scared. But she nodded at Tony, and they strode side by side across the open yard to the grape arbor.

"Hmmm..." Tony felt the soil. "The big man has certainly been doing something here. The dirt's loose, not packed down at all. I can feel the perimeters of the hole where the ground is solid all the way around. This will be easy." And with that, Tony commenced digging.

Katy tiptoed several feet away and lowered herself the ground, staring at the house. She had a terrible feeling, like she had forgotten something or that something was wrong and she just didn't know it yet. Dirt flew behind her as Tony applied himself industriously to the task, when suddenly bright lights flooded the back yard and Katy knew what she had forgotten.

The big man's driveway ran past the carport and the rose hedge to a shed at the rear of the property. A tall truck blaring loud music blundered into the driveway. The passenger door opened and the big man swung out, slammed the door, and watched the obnoxious vehicle plow backwards into the street and lurch off into the night. He stumbled upon the carport, pointed a flashlight across his back yard, and froze at the sight of the partially excavated hole and the two ingrates who were meddling in his business. He let out a drunken roar and charged. Tony and Katy fled in opposite directions.

Katy reached the safety of the undergrowth that defined the

rear property line. Tony, confused by the abrupt noise and light and by what he had uncovered, ran blindly toward what he thought to be a dark, safe haven. He dashed straight into the big man's shed. The big man swung the door shut behind him and slid the bolt through its frame, trapping Tony inside. The shed had no windows and only one door. The floor was solid concrete. The big man laughed as he walked away.

A very long time later, Tony heard movement by the shed door and prepared to attack. In the pitch darkness he could see nothing, but he would not go down without putting up a fight the big man would not soon forget.

"Tony! Tony, are you okay in there?"

"Katy! Thank goodness he didn't get you, too! Can you get me out of here?"

"Shhhh!" Katy hissed. "Keep your voice down! I might be able to figure out how the lock works if I can get to it." Katy stretched and extended her arms. "It's just out of reach."

"It can't be," Tony said. "Katy, I've got to get out of here. I believe the woman is still alive."

"But I watched the big man cover her back up! That's why I couldn't come to you sooner. He went into the house less than an hour ago."

"I swear I saw the tarp moving, as if she were breathing," Tony said. "If she is still alive, it's more important than ever that we get her out of there. If we don't do it soon, it really will be too late."

Katy looked around desperately. "Wait!" she exclaimed. "There's a tricycle in the driveway next door! If I can push it over here and stand on it, I might be able to slide back the bolt and open the door!"

The tricycle weighed much more than Katy, and a strip of thick grass grew between the neighbor's driveway and the big man's shed. Katy struggled with the awkward thing until she was exhausted. It took over an hour to position the tricycle beneath the lock.

Katy climbed onto the unsteady frame, balancing as best she

could. She reached for the bolt and tugged on it once, twice – with a series of uneven jerks, Katy worked it open. She leaped off the tricycle, stepped back from the shed, and heaved a weary sigh.

"Okay, Tony. You can come out now."

Tony charged out of the shed, flinging back the door and hurling the tricycle back into its own lawn.

"It will be morning soon," Katy said.

"We don't have much time," Tony agreed. "Come on! Forget keeping a lookout. You need to help me dig."

The unlikely pair ran across the yard and began digging in earnest, one on each side of the shallow grave. Dawn spread gray streaks across the sky as Tony unearthed the tarp. He pulled at the stubborn material, trying to expose the woman's face. Katy joined him in the effort, and together they tore it apart. Just a little more...

They were so intent on their task that neither of them noticed the danger they were in. Katy was yanked off her feet and dangling in mid-air before they realized the big man had come out of the house. He held her aloft until she screamed, and he cuffed her hard until she shrank into a hurt, terrified silence. Tony hesitated at the edge of the garden, torn between helping Katy and saving the big man's wife. But the big man did not intend that Tony should do either one. He crushed Katy under one arm and reached behind his back with the other, retrieving a pistol from his waistband. Tony saw it coming and fled for his life.

The morning hours crawled miserably by. Tony did not go home. He crouched in the shrubbery against Katy's house and watched as the sitter searched and called for Katy, became upset that Katy didn't answer, and left for church. Tony ventured across the street twice, but the big man occupied a lawn chair in the back yard both times. He had buried the woman again. Katy was nowhere to be seen. Tony shuddered at the thought of what might have happened to her.

When families began arriving home from church, Tony crossed the street again and looked through the rose hedge into the big man's back yard. Chicken wire now covered the grave.

The big man had finally gone. And Katy...

Tony started to leap over the hedge when he remembered the shed. He went to the door. It had been bolted tight again, but was easy for Tony to unfasten. Katy lay on the concrete floor, eyes bulging and tongue protruding, dying of slow strangulation from a rope tied viciously tight around her throat. Her breath came in weak gasps, and Tony knew she was exhausted to the point of giving up.

Without a word he began working at the rope. The knot pressed so tight against Katy's windpipe that Tony could hardly grasp it. His talents were of strength and brute power, not in tedious and delicate pursuits, but he did not give up. Within minutes Tony flung the rope aside. He carried Katy out of the building and into the undergrowth at the rear of the big man's yard. He rested there with her until mid-afternoon, when she was able to stand and walk without losing her balance.

At length she cleared her throat and spoke in a raspy whisper. "We have to try again. If the woman isn't already dead, she won't last much longer."

"I'll go," Tony said. "You stay here and wait for me."

"No," Katy objected. "I'm the one who got us into this. We will see it through together."

They marched straight to the arbor, not trying to hide anymore. Neighbors socialized in adjoining yards, enjoying the early spring sunshine, and birds sang overhead. Tony took hold of the chicken wire and threw his weight back, pulling the flimsy metal stakes out of the soft earth. Katy began scooping dirt from above the woman's face before he finished.

Working side by side, they once again uncovered the woman's upper body. Tony took hold of the tarp and yanked forcefully, ripping it away from the woman's face. Her eyes were closed and her lips were blue, but...Katy leaned over her face...

"You were right, Tony! She's breathing! The woman is alive!"

A door slammed and a drunk man roared. He charged his adversaries with the shovel. Tony dodged and ran, but Katy stumbled, still incredibly weak from being strangled. The shovel caught her broadside, and Tony watched in horror as her body sailed into the underbrush and landed with a crash.

But their mission was accomplished. Curious neighbors peered across the hedge to see what the ruckus was about. They saw the big man with his shovel standing beside the open grave containing his partially buried wife wrapped in a torn and dirty tarp. One neighbor ran to call an ambulance. Another ran to call the police. Still another ran to call her cousin who worked for the local newspaper. The rest of them broke through the rose hedge to stand and stare at the drunken felon and his unconscious wife.

In all the commotion, no one paid attention to the massive rottweiler snuffling frantically through the brush until he came upon a limp tuft of calico fur. He nuzzled it, pawed at it, and lifted it ever so tenderly in his huge jaws. Holding his head high, Tony cut through the yard on the opposite side of the big man's house to avoid detection, hurried across the street to Katy's house, and deposited her gently behind the shrubbery.

"Katy?" He prodded her with nose. "Come on, Katy, wake up, now."

Katy's eyes remained closed, and Tony had to place his muzzle against her face just to make sure she was breathing.

"Katy, please." Tony licked the tangled fur and whimpered. "Please, Katy, wake up, come on, now…"

Katy regained consciousness by degrees, as though surfacing gradually through a thick syrup. She could hear Tony calling, his voice sounding closer, closer…

She opened her eyes and cried out at the sight of Tony's huge face looming over hers. He backed up, and she saw the relief in his eyes.

Katy tried to sit up. "Eow," she said softly, squeezing her eyes against the pain. "I hurt all over. What happened?"

"We did good, Katy," Tony moved next to her so she could lean against his leg. "The woman is alive. She will be taken care of, and the big man will be punished for what he did to her. Do you hear them?"

Approaching sirens announced the arrival of an ambulance

and of law enforcement vehicles that surrounded the big man's house. Tony watched from the shrubbery, reciting a play-by-play for Katy, nuzzling her once in a while to make sure she was okay. As the last police car drove away, a familiar vehicle pulled into Katy's driveway.

"Hey," Tony said. "Looks like your mom and dad are home."

Katy sighed with relief. She wanted nothing more than to nestle into Mom's perfect lap and enjoy the ecstasy of a good chin-scratching from Dad. But first...

Katy looked up at her lifelong enemy. "Tony," she began, but he shook his head.

"Save it, kid," he said gruffly. "I mean, this doesn't change anything, you know. We're still the same as we always were. We don't want to forget that. People might get the wrong idea."

Katy looked at him and smiled her superior smile. "Sure, Tony. Whatever you say."

Tony didn't mind Katy's smile. It was...well, it was Katy. Tony did his best to smile in return.

Miss May met Mom and Dad in the front yard and followed them into the house, explaining something in a low, repentant voice. Mom and Dad ran back out almost immediately.

"Oh, Wes, what if she's hurt!" Mom cried. "I knew we shouldn't have left her for a whole weekend!"

Kibble rattled in a bowl, and Katy jumped at the sound. "Where's my Katy?" Dad called. "Come here, Katy!"

"Here, Katy-Katy-Katy!" Mom joined in.

Katy looked up at Tony. Tony looked down at Katy. She stood, stretched gingerly, and walked out of the shrubbery to the front porch. Mom immediately whisked her up and commented on her poor messy fur and her tired little body and we-are-so-sorry-we-left-you-for-so-long. Katy snuggled into Mom's arms, touched her nose to Dad's cheek, and laid her chin over Mom's shoulder as Mom carried her into the house.

As Dad held the door open, Katy looked toward the shrubbery and briefly closed both eyes in a slow, acquiescent blink. The shrubbery gently swayed as a tail thumped the ground. A great

nose lowered, and warm eyes looked up.
  The door closed behind Katy.
  Tony turned and headed home.

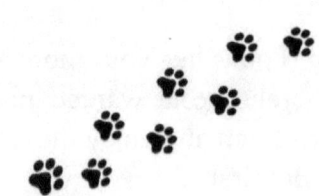

Into The Wind

"Storm coming."

Motzie watched Galen lift his head high and widen his nostrils like a hound dog pup scenting for a rabbit. "What does a storm smell like?"

"Like a storm, of course."

Motzie squinted at the sky. Wisps escaped since morning from her ponytail danced across her face in the breeze, tickling her nose and interfering with her study. She impatiently tucked them behind her ears. "But what is that *like*?"

"A cantaloupe smells like a cantaloupe," Galen informed her. "A skunk smells like a skunk. A storm smells like a storm."

Motzie lowered her gaze from the clear blue to Galen's weathered grimace. "When will it get here?"

"'Bout midafternoon, most likely."

"How can you tell?"

"Just can."

Motzie stifled a disappointed sigh. "Oh."

Galen read her with a glance. "Some things are hard to explain. You learn and come to understand. That's not the same as knowing. You can understand lots of things that don't come with descriptions and instructions."

Motzie brightened. "Like how dumplings don't feel like they

look or taste like they feel. Or how the sun takes hold of your back on a hot day."

Galen squeezed his eyes like a cat and pressed his lips together.

Motzie smiled, too. She dug at a rock. It was too big for her to carry, but she hoisted it anyway and turned toward the wagon only to stagger into Galen's large, rough hands. Her arms went suddenly light as he relieved her of the rock.

"Don't do that. You'll hurt your back."

Motzie hung her head and reached for her hoe.

The force of the rock landing in the wagon caused a small avalanche against all four sides. "Everything you do causes other things to happen." Galen nodded at the skittering stones relocating within the four-walled boundary. "You hurt your back, now, and you won't be fit to help me or Maw out. Our burdens would be added to by having to take care of you."

"I was only trying to do a good job."

"You'll do better when you learn to manage your pride. Wanting to do things all by yourself is fine to the extent you're able. When you're facing something too big for you to handle alone, be brave enough to admit it and ask somebody to help you. Strength and courage shine when you admit your weakness."

Motzie shook her head. "How can a person look strong when he's weak?"

Galen pressed his lips together again, and Motzie realized this was another one of those things that she would, somehow, grow to understand.

At noon, they washed their arms up to their elbows in a galvanized tub full of rainwater and dried them on a raspy towel hanging from a loop of wire on the corner of the smokehouse. Motzie heard a flutter and looked up at a sparrow sitting on the dinner bell that had called them home moments before.

"She has a nest under the eave." Motzie pointed to straws protruding from under the smokehouse roof.

"Dangerous," Galen said. "Ornery birds, mice, chipmunks. They can cause fire." He upended a crate and stood to reach the nest. The sparrow twittered in fear and flew away to the clothesline, alighting to watch.

"Are you going to tear out her nest?" Motzie watched the bird flutter along the clothesline and was sorry she had betrayed its home.

Galen stepped off the crate and pushed it aside. "There are eggs. Three of 'em. Reckon we can oblige Missus Sparrow until they're hatched."

Motzie exhaled with relief and hurried alongside Galen to the house. It was her turn to scent the air as they approached the kitchen door. "Fried chicken." She stopped short. "Are we expecting company?"

Galen turned and looked her full in the face. "Hawse is here."

Motzie went still on the outside. On the inside all the parts that usually fit so neatly and held together so well erupted and swirled about in a maelstrom of emotion. *I could go back,* Motzie thought vaguely, *and work in the field until he's gone.* But Galen wouldn't let her. She might pick up a heavy rock again and hurt her back, and then she'd be alone with no one to help her to the house. *I could just say I'm not hungry and spend the afternoon in my room.* That would be a lie in the first place. Motzie was starved. In the second place, Grandma wouldn't let her get away with doing such a prissy thing. Motzie cast a desperate glance at Galen, and Galen caught it and soothed it and offered the only suggestion at his disposal.

"Take it easy, Motzie. He won't stay long. We'll go back to the field right after dinner. By the time we come home for supper, he'll be long gone."

What choice did she have, so Motzie trailed Galen through the kitchen door and stood behind him with her gaze fixed on the table, trying to appear unconcerned at the strange familiar voice rising and falling from the corner where the wood stove sat in the winter. *I could have run around the house and gone through the front door,* she thought. *I could have run to my room and combed my hair and put on a dress.* But she was filthy from working in the field. A Sunday dress and braids tied with ribbons wouldn't disguise the dirt, and there wasn't time for a bath. At least her hands and face were clean. She tucked wisps behind her ears again and pulled her ponytail tight.

"Somebody's behind you," the voice observed to Galen. "Who might that be?"

"Well, who do you think?" Grandma's voice flowed with the timbre of inexorable reality. The current pushed Motzie from behind Galen as it pulled him a step in the opposite direction. She stood adrift and wishing with all her might for somebody, somebody...

"Look here, Motzie, what's so interesting out the window that it can't wait another minute? Look who's here." Grandma's voice reprimanded and commanded and hurt, oh, how it hurt.

Motzie obeyed. Motzie looked. Hawse appeared much the same as the last time she'd seen him two years ago, though two years equaled eternity to a ten-year-old, one-fifth of her whole life, and Motzie found herself comparing Hawse then to Hawse now. Then, blue shirt. Now white. Then, brown pants. Now gray. Then, sandy hair. Now dishwater beige. Then: she looked at his face. She remembered a wide smile. Grandma said women found Hawse handsome for his wide smile and ocean blue eyes. Now the smile framed white teeth. Motzie had never seen the ocean, but if those aging eyes reflected its color, it couldn't be all that much to look at. The main thing Motzie remembered about Hawse was a loud, domineering laugh that made children and dogs cower while adults fidgeted with discomfort. Motzie remembered that laugh because it had been directed at her and because somewhere inside of her amidst the tumult of churning emotions a spot remained tender and sore, like a bruise.

Hawse looked her over with the detached assessment a farmer might pass across a heifer over which he was feigning interest for the benefit of an audience, though he had no intention of following through with the purchase. His study was critical and brief. "Matilda." He moved the word around in his mouth. "What have you been doing this morning, girl?"

Motzie swallowed grief and fear and called forth that pride

Galen had warned her about. "I've been helping Uncle Galen clear the field up by the branch."

"Clear a field. How exactly does a little girl clear a field?"

Motzie wanted to beseech Galen with her eyes, wanted to run. Wished for once it were September instead of July so she could take refuge in school all day and not even know he had stopped by. Wished she had fallen in the field and been crushed by that big rock. Wished the avalanche had poured over her and buried her safely from sight. "We're hauling away the rocks and cutting down the thicket." Motzie watched his face and saw it coming. This is what she remembered about Hawse. This is how she knew him.

Hawse sat still as though holding his breath until laughter forced its way through his lips in a hoarse bark. "Good job, Galen. You'll make a man out of her yet." He turned the haughty laughter on his mother. "Thought you'd have done better by her than that. Does she sew, does she cook? Do anything that girls do? Heck, if I'd have known she'd turn out to be such a good boy, I'd have raised her myself." He offered Motzie his wide, mocking grin. Motzie didn't find him handsome at all. "Do you smoke?"

The bruise hurt. Motzie needed to go somewhere and cry.

"Hawse! Of course she doesn't smoke." Grandma chided him breathlessly, out of her element and needing to regain control of the atmosphere within her own kitchen. "Let's all get to the table now before our dinner gets cold. Motzie, you may sit beside your father."

"Yes, Matilda," Hawse parroted. "You may sit beside your father."

Grandma's look of reproach and Galen's dark anger did not make Motzie feel any better. She could tell that neither of them would challenge Hawse. Hawse knew it, too, and relaxed in the contentment of easy authority. Motzie would rather sit beside him than across from him. She didn't want to see his face. Hawse swung into a chair. Motzie perched on a chair next to him. Grandma and Galen took their seats across the table.

"Galen, would you lead us," Grandma requested. She, Galen,

and Motzie bowed their heads for a brief prayer. Motzie tried to concentrate on Galen's blessing and ignore the movement and noise of Hawse. At Galen's 'amen' they opened their eyes to find Hawse devouring the largest piece of chicken and cramming down a plateful of food as fast as he could push it onto his fork with a biscuit.

Grandma put her hands to her face. "Hawse, we were praying!"

"Your loss." He held up his piece of chicken, leered at his mother, and sank his teeth into the meat. He tore off a huge chunk and chewed loudly. "I got the last pickle, too."

Grandma rose from the table and walked outside.

"All the more for us, aye?" Hawse grinned companionably at Galen.

"She's gone to the cellar for another jar of pickles," Galen informed him. "She'll be right back."

"Too bad," Hawse ruminated. "But then, one old woman won't eat much." He helped himself to another piece of chicken and two more biscuits.

Motzie watched him rake the last of the mashed potatoes out onto his plate and drown them in gravy. Grandma's mashed potatoes were her favorite, and she hadn't had a single bite of them. She looked across the table at Galen, but Galen focused on his plate. He finally looked up at her as though angry that she had made him do so.

"Get to eating," he ordered. "We have a lot of work to do this afternoon."

Hawse opened his mouth to comment, but Grandma interrupted when she entered with two jars of pickles. "For me?" He leaned back in his chair and guffawed, exposing a mouthful of half-chewed food.

"You've had yours," Grandma said evenly, "and most of ours as well."

Motzie gaped at the rejoinder. Galen slid his eyes toward his mother in admiration. Hawse flinched as though stung. His eyes narrowed and his chewing slowed, but did not stop, as the constantly-moving fork ensured his mouth stayed full.

"Here, Motzie." Grandma took a bowl from the oven and held it beside Motzie's plate. It was filled with mashed potatoes. Motzie looked up in surprise at her grandmother's understanding nod. "I know you're fond of them. I'll hold the bowl while you serve yourself. It's too hot to set on the table."

"I got room for some of them on my plate," Hawse sang out. "Just bring 'em on over here when you've fed the kid."

"You've had yours," Grandma repeated. Hawse watched as she held the bowl for Galen, served herself, and placed the empty bowl in the sink.

"Not a very gracious hostess, are you?" Hawse smirked. "But I can't hold you too accountable. Don't imagine you all get many visitors out here at the backside of nowhere. You probably don't know things about manners and treating guests with proper etiquette."

Grandma ignored him, consuming her meal with slow dignity that made her son's gluttony all the more reminiscent of a hog at slop. Galen laid his fork and knife diagonally across his plate, drank down the last of his milk, and wiped his mouth with a napkin. He looked across at the table Motzie. She finished her mashed potatoes and green beans in three neat bites, swallowed two gulps of milk, and sat up straight.

"Motzie and I'd best get back to work," Galen said. "See you later, Maw." He kissed Grandma on top of her head as he rose from the table.

Motzie sprang from her chair and flew to Galen's side. "Love you, Grandma."

"Love you, darlin'. Watch her, Galen."

"What about me? Don't you love your dear old dad?" Hawse directed an indignant frown at Motzie. "Running off and leaving me, just like that, without even the courtesy of a goodbye. I'm hurt."

Motzie froze. Galen placed a comforting hand on her shoulder.

Hawse swallowed and smeared at his mouth with a napkin. "I

know what. I'll forgive your rudeness, inexcusable as it is, if you'll come over here and give me a kiss." He leaned toward her and presented a cheek. "Right here." He tapped the side of his face with his fork.

Motzie felt Galen's hand tighten on her shoulder. She looked to Grandma for help. Grandma sipped her iced tea and looked at Motzie as though all of life were suddenly founded on practicality and common sense. "Go kiss your father, Motzie, and then you may leave with Galen."

"Come kiss your father, Matilda," Hawse lilted.

Galen gave her shoulder a little squeeze and released her. *Wish the avalanche had poured over her and buried her safely from sight...* Motzie forced her feet to carry her around the table to the chair she had previously occupied. She stopped behind the chair and leaned as far as she could toward Hawse, unwilling to approach any closer. As she touched her lips to his cheek, Hawse abruptly turned, clapped a hand behind her head and kissed her fully, wet and rough, on the mouth.

Motzie struggled, suffocating, clamping her teeth together as he tried to force his tongue into her mouth. She heard her grandmother's shriek and Galen's outraged roar, and then she was wrenched away and carried by her arms outside onto the porch to the tune of Hawse's bellowing laughter. She stood on the concrete step alone, sobbing, scrubbing at her bruised lips with the backs of her hands, crying so hard she couldn't spit out the taste, the smell, the brutality, the betrayal that was Hawse. She was aware of Grandma's high-pitched tirade punctuated by Galen's bass rebuke. Then the hoe slid through Motzie's sweaty hands, the blade rang sharp against a stone, the stone magnified the gravity that pulled her arms, her body, her being down to the dusty, clod-rutted earth. The stone arced through the air in slow motion to land on the heap in the wagon, causing a small avalanche against all four sides. *Everything you do causes other things to happen.* She nodded at the skittering stones relocating within the four-walled boundary.

The first rumble of thunder troubled the sky at three o'clock.

Wind responded to the cue with a sudden gust that nearly took Motzie off her feet. She leaned on her hoe into the wind and looked for Galen. He stood straight and tall on the other side of the wagon, breathing the wind right down into his lungs, addressing the sky with eyes that acknowledged what it told him and heeded its advice.

"We'd best get to the house."

Motzie was not afraid of the wind and the clouds and the solitude. She stood as straight as Galen and looked him as squarely in the face. "I'll stand the storm."

"No need. He's gone," Galen replied.

"How do you know that?"

Galen tossed his hoe into the wagon and climbed aboard the tractor. He held out a hand to Motzie. "He's gone."

She studied his face. She couldn't recall any reason at all not to trust Galen. "I'll ride in the wagon."

"The rocks will roll around. You might get hurt."

Motzie tossed her hoe atop the pile beside Galen's and took his hand. She stood on the narrow running board to his left and grasped the round metal bar that served as an arm rest in a white-knuckled grip. Galen started the tractor and observed the placement of Motzie's feet and hands. The tractor gave a lurch and crept forward across the field. Motzie watched the rocks in the wagon. They did indeed roll around, jarred loose by every rut and bump in the field. Motzie was glad her ankles were not at their mercy, and she was grateful to Galen for offering his wisdom in her favor. Galen drove at a snail's pace. Motzie wished he would go faster, but she knew he wouldn't, not with her on the tractor. He'd heard of too many farming accidents, he'd tell her, where children were hurt or killed. Galen wouldn't share the first detail about any of them, but she had fallen silent before his assertion enough times to know better than to ask again. If the implications were uncertain, Galen's concern for her was not, and she basked in the daily manifestations of fatherly care he bestowed upon her.

The tractor carried them across the field out onto a gravel lane, which in turn meandered slowly across the farm toward home. They passed the tobacco barn and came in sight of the tool shed, a long stable for farm implements. Galen stopped in front of it and shut off the tractor. Motzie jumped down and ran to look for doodlebugs while Galen unhitched the wagon. She found a series of craters of varying sizes in the dirt just where she knew they'd be, little funnels made of dust, each with a doodlebug in the bottom waiting for an ant to slip over the rim and slide down into its waiting jaws. Ant lions, Galen called them. Motzie thought that sounded wicked and murderous. Calling them doodlebugs made them much more friendly. She captured one of the tiny predators once in a while by delicately flicking dirt down the side of a funnel and scooping up the doodlebug as it surfaced, kicking more dirt in order to thwart its prey's escape. She held the soft little dust-colored body in her hand, laughed when it tried to root down into the crevice between her fingers, released it and watched it disappear under the dirt. Her friend Sally told her that if she knelt beside the craters and called, "Doodlebug, doodlebug, your house is on fire!" over and over, the whole lot of them would eventually come puffing forth from the bottoms of their funnels. Motzie had never had success with that. Flicking little scatterings of dust into a single crater, mimicking a hapless ant, that's how to catch a doodlebug. There wouldn't be time today. Galen had already backed the tractor into the shed. She swept a farewell glance across the ant lion village and trotted to catch up with her uncle as he walked down the lane toward home.

Thunder rumbled louder, vibrating the ground under their feet. Her ponytail was a mess anyway, so Motzie unhooked the rubber band from the plastic clip and released her hair to the mercy of the wind. A jagged bolt of lightning stood on two legs beyond the trees across the farm. Motzie stared where it had appeared, fascinated, until another bolt reached through the sky and touched the earth with six fingers. It ripped the sky and ripped her heart, and she felt the shuddering resonance of its contact with the earth down to the very core of her being.

Galen looked back for her. "Come on."

Great drops of water smacked the ground with splotches as big as her palm. Motzie ran to keep up with Galen's long stride all the way to the house and up the steps under the porch. They paused by the kitchen door to look back into the deluge, as though the porch roof somehow protected them from every danger. Motzie watched a moth flutter amidst the roses on the trellis, careening from leaf to bloom to stem. She wondered if moths ever accidentally impaled themselves on thorns. She watched Galen watch the sky, and when she looked for the moth again it was nowhere to be seen.

Grandma joined them on the porch, stumbling out the door with her apron clutched in both fists. Her dress was torn, and her hair sprang wildly from the usually tidy bun. She looked at Galen, and something was terribly wrong, and Motzie saw that Grandma wasn't wearing her false teeth. The sunken lips weren't as frightening as the sunken eyes. The skin around her left eye swelled blue-black from brow to cheekbone and the white part of the eye on the left side was red all the way to the iris. Motzie backed away. Grandma's eye was bleeding. But no blood leaked from the left eye no matter how many times or how hard Grandma blinked. Galen turned to his mother and a shadow darkened his features with a more frightening promise than Motzie had ever seen in most tormented sky.

"He won't bother us again." Grandma said to Galen. She lisped without her teeth. "He won't hurt Motzie anymore."

And then Grandma and Galen did something Motzie had never seen either of them do. Galen wrapped his arms around Grandma, and she hid her face against his chest and sobbed.

Motzie ran into the house to get a handkerchief for her grandmother. She went straight to the dresser drawer and opened it and stared at the butcher knife lying so oddly out of place amidst the lacy linens. The knife must have been dirty, because the blade was discolored, and deep red stains had rubbed off on Grandma's handkerchiefs and soiled every last one. Motzie closed the drawer and ran back to the kitchen. She took a clean dish cloth out onto the porch and gently dabbed at her grandmother's cheeks. Grandma's face crumpled like wadded tissue and she trembled violently, and Motzie was shocked to realize for the first time in her life that her grandmother was old. Black and blue splotches discolored her arms, and the fragile, parchment skin had torn and bled in several places. An ugly purple bruise encircled her neck. Motzie tried to take Grandma's face in her hands, not understanding what had happened, but wanting to touch the wound and heal the hurt. But Grandma turned her face away and hid again in the folds of Galen's shirt.

"I'm sorry, Maw," Galen murmured, and Motzie experienced another shock at the tears falling from Galen's eyes into his mother's hair. "God knows I'm so sorry. If I'd had any idea he'd have gone this far, I'd never have left you here alone with him. I was afraid for Motzie. I never thought he'd hurt you. I'd kill him before I'd let him hurt you."

"Don't matter," Grandma insisted from somewhere very far away. "Don't matter. Like father, like son. Fruit rotten from the womb. Better me than Motzie. Better me than you. I won't have to live with it long."

The world fell silent with her. The rain and wind died away. Motzie looked across the yard, and it was like viewing the world through a green lens.

"Let's get you to the hospital." Galen drew back.

The first marbles of hail bounced off the roof and along the sidewalk.

"No." Grandma straightened and looked out at the storm with renewed hope. "No, I'll go to my new home from my old one."

"Maw, don't talk like that," Galen reprimanded. "You're hurt bad. That's why we have to get you to the hospital where they can fix you up. Come on, now."

"Some things can't be fixed," Grandma lisped. "He's gone, Galen. I need to go, too."

The pounding of the hail became underscored with an ominous rumble that didn't fade away.

"The thunder's constant," Motzie said. "It's getting louder."

"The cellar," Galen ordered. "Get to the cellar, Motzie, now!"

Motzie ran ahead and hauled the heavy cellar door upward with all her might. Galen lifted Grandma in his arms and carried her down the steps. He sat her gently on a crate and hurried back up the steps to help Motzie lower and latch the door.

"What is it?" Motzie begged. "Uncle Galen, please! What is happening?"

"It's just a storm, Motzie." The gentle voice permeated her spirit just as the thunder had pierced it earlier. The tumult of her shattered self instantly slowed, calmed, began to settle into place. Hawse really was gone. Grandma had said so. Motzie looked at the broken, aged rag doll weeping on the crate and wondered exactly what Grandma had meant by that.

"It's just a storm," Galen said again. He upended a bucket in front of the freezer and sat down beside his mother. He slid a second crate alongside his bucket and reached for Motzie. "Come here. Sit with me."

Motzie felt thunder all around them and in them. The house vibrated as though a train were rolling through. She curled up small against Galen and looked up only once to see Grandma huddled under his other arm. Good thing Galen was so strong. Why had Hawse hurt Grandma? She flinched at a series of crashes overhead.

"Take it easy, Motzie. Have faith. It's only a storm. Storms can be rough while they last, but they don't last long."

But this one lasted for a very long time, and Motzie finally fell asleep to the skirmish of rain and wind and Galen's heartbeat and Grandma's tears.

Shimmer

She was drying dishes when she got the news, swirling a towel inside a bright pink bowl when the doorbell rang. She glanced at the clock, wondering for the hundredth time what was taking Payt so long. It was almost six-thirty. He should have been home an hour ago.

She tossed the towel aside, wiping her hands on the sides of her shirt as she reluctantly answered the door. *Please, not another window salesman, political activist, or fundraising enthusiast peddling overpriced products...*

She opened the door, a brief speech ready, and stared at the police officer waiting on her front porch.

"Gloria Spencer?" he asked.

She nodded, mentally switching gears from her original assumption to the vaguely disturbing reality.

"Mrs. Payton Spencer?" the policeman ventured further.

"He's not home right now," she blurted. "He had to stop by the grocery to pick up some things for supper, and he's not home...yet..."

The officer solemnly lowered his eyes, and Gloria realized that she was barefoot and her toenail polish was flaking off, and she got embarrassed and invited him into the house.

He followed her into the living room, removing his hat on the way. Gloria gestured toward the wing chair as she perched on the sofa, but the officer remained standing. He paused for a moment beside the photographs on the mantle and cleared his throat.

"Mrs. Spencer, I am so sorry." He glanced down at the hat in his hands, tracing the badge with a fingertip before lifting his eyes to her unwavering gaze. "Payton Spencer was involved in a motor vehicle collision at the South Mulberry exit about thirty minutes ago."

Gloria didn't blink.

"There were no survivors."

Gloria stared at the man as though he had begun a riveting story and she could hardly wait to hear how it ended. Her expression did not change. The officer was a model of quiet composure and professional empathy. Was there anything he could do for her – contact a neighbor, call a family member to come over, drive her to a friend's house.

Gloria answered his questions and said she was fine...turned down the courteous offers, no, she would be fine...walked him to the door and thanked him, of all things, for coming by, and insisted that she was going to be fine...

The officer gave a sympathetic smile and wished her well as he stepped out onto the porch. Gloria closed the door behind him and watched through a pane of etched glass as he climbed into his cruiser and drove away.

And she was alone. Just like that.

"Do it again, Daddy!"

Little Gloria clapped her hands and twirled around her father's legs as he performed a comical dance and sang, "Glow, little glow worm, shine and shimmer..."

He never used her full name. The moment a nurse placed the tiny girl infant in his arms, her father smiled into the face of his very own miracle and told the nurses that no day would ever be a dark day again, because there would always be a Glo in his life.

The nurses laughed. Her father cried.

When she was a child, her father's charming song sounded larger than life, and she tried hard to live up to its words. When she felt happy, she could produce a beautiful smile that might be said to fairly shine; but how, Gloria would wonder, does one *shimmer*? Sometimes Gloria still found herself mimicking her father's steps and wondering whether there really was an answer, embarrassed that such childish thoughts should challenge the maturity of her mind.

By the time Gloria realized the telephone was ringing, the caller had given up. The display smoothly scrolled the number of the hospital.

Gloria changed her clothes and got her purse and drove to the hospital feeling foolish, as though humoring a pretense that amounted to nothing more than a horrible waste of time – someone's idea of a monstrous practical joke.

An impassive older woman in a taut blouse and skirt faced her from the other side of a stark countertop and asked questions Gloria never thought she'd have to answer. Greenway Funeral Home. Valiant Health and Life Insurance. Sign this here and that there. The woman began to explain about autopsies and organ donor programs.

Oh, dear God…

The woman handed her a little sack and Gloria wandered out to the parking garage and somehow found her car.

She should call someone. Her parents should be the first to know. Payton was the son they never had. She didn't want to say those words, see their faces, feel their grief, but they should hear it from her, and by tomorrow rumors would be all over town. Gloria visited her mother and father and broke the news and held them as they cried.

Payton's parents had died soon after he and Gloria were married. Like Gloria, Payt was an only child. A handful of cousins were scattered about the country like chaff in the wind. There was no one close. Her mother would spread the news to those who needed to hear it. Gloria wouldn't have to do that again.

Evening had faded to nightfall when she went home, against her parents' objections, to be alone. Shadows overtook the front lawn. A few impatient stars pierced the overcast sky. Gloria stepped inside her house and lingered by the front door. She gazed around the living room. Darkness had fallen all at once.

The kitchen light projected a bright, crooked rectangle on the carpet outside the doorway. Oh, yes, the dishes. Gloria mechanically walked to the kitchen. She placed the little sack on the counter and pushed it back against the wall. The towel lay where she had left it, a damp heap beside a bright pink bowl. She glanced at the clock. Three hours had passed, almost to the minute. *Glow, little glow worm...* Where does time go?

The dishes had dried on the rack. Gloria wiped them with the towel anyway and put them away until only the bright pink bowl remained. Gloria couldn't look at the bowl, couldn't face reality, not yet...she glanced at the clock again. It was ten p.m. and where was Payt, oh, where was her beloved husband...

Gloria stayed busy and shut the doors of her mind. She did a load of laundry and hung Payton's shirts neat and straight in the closet. She diced apples, oranges, grapes, and bananas to make the fresh fruit salad he so adored. At last she bathed, shampooed, brushed her teeth, and sat in front of the television to wait. It was after midnight. Payton was working late, she decided. He would slip into bed beside her when he got home and hold her tight because he had missed her so. She would smile and snuggle against his chest and breathe in his wonderful scent as she drifted back to sleep.

Gloria turned off the television and went to bed and waited. Sleep taunted her until tiring of the game, and dreams carried her unwillingly away.

"Daddy, do animals go to Heaven when they die?"
"No, honey, they sure don't."

"Why not?"

"Because animals don't have souls. God only gave souls to people, so only people can go to Heaven."

"But why, Daddy? Smoky was a good dog. I want him to go to Heaven, too!"

"People are special to God, Glo. Very special. He watches over His animals, but He loves us more than any of them. See, some parts of the world God commanded into existence, and some things He made. But people He *created*, Glo."

Though she could not fully accept her father's explanation, Gloria fell silent before the reverence and awe in his voice. She stared down at the collie-sized grave, keenly feeling her loss, until her father laid his hand on her shoulder.

"And because animals don't have an afterlife, people need to make their time on earth as pleasant as possible. You took good care of Smoky and made him very happy while he was alive. I'm sure God is proud of you for that."

The phone rang sharply and Gloria bolted upright in bed. It was daylight already! She hadn't heard the alarm go off. Payton must have forgotten to set it.

She reached across the bed for the phone, ignoring the vast empty space beside her.

"Gloria? Hey, this is Roger," came the cheerful voice of Payton's best friend. "Say, did you kick the old boy out of the house on time this morning? He's not at his desk and no one has seen him come in."

A fist closed around her lungs and her heart. Someone had punched her hard in the stomach and left her gasping for air…

She had assumed everyone would know.

"He won't be in today, all right, Roger? I'll explain later. Tell Sherry to call me tonight."

She quietly put down the receiver, got out of bed, got dressed. Called her employer to tell him she wouldn't be at work without explaining why. Vaguely managed a wisp of gratitude for small favors when the tone of his voice indicated he already knew. She had barely hung up the phone when Mr. Greenway called and invited her to visit his office within the hour.

Gloria took Payton's best suit – really, his only suit – from the closet and matched a shirt, tie, socks, and underwear. She zipped everything inside a nylon bag and drove to the funeral home. From a distance, she answered more abstract questions that could not possibly apply to her life for many years to come. Lighthouse Baptist Church and cemetery. Roger, of course, and Tony and Dave, and Evan and Garrett and Joel. Sherry had a beautiful voice. If she would be willing to sing…

Gloria left the aquatic colors of Mr. Greenway's office wondering why so many funeral parlors were named green or decorated in shades of green. She drifted through a series of asinine errands that would have been accorded tremendous importance the day before, and then she went home and wandered aimlessly from one silent room to another.

A little paper sack waited patiently on the kitchen counter. Gloria opened it with trembling hands and reached inside. A small cold thing greeted her touch. Gloria stared at the object in the palm of her hand, hyperventilating, pleading against reality that forced itself upon her until she was too weak to fight back. She snatched the pink bowl from beside the sink and hurled it into the wall, screaming her lungs empty again and again until she sank, exhausted, to the kitchen floor, wracked with helpless sobs of grief too great to ever bear, clutching to her chest the wedding band that had not left her husband's hand since the day they sealed their vows at the altar of Lighthouse Baptist Church.

The church was less than a mile from home. The cemetery ascended the hill behind the chapel, peaked against the clouds, and scattered tombstones down the other side.

Payton Spencer was buried in that cemetery, just out of sight beyond the crest of the hill. Children ran to play in the city park across the street while their parents proceeded to the gravesite.

Gloria listened to their laughter and lifted her face to the afternoon sun, wondering how the day could possibly be so beautiful and people so joyful when life as she knew it was over.

And in more ways than she could have imagined. Long days soon became weeks that slipped by as unnoticed as Gloria had become. Married friends drifted away, uncomfortable with the crushed apparition that reminded them of what they, too, might become, but for the grace of God. Coworkers made polite conversation as they avoided her eyes and her pain. Gloria's parents called every night and visited often. But nothing could stop the fog from rolling in to claim her spirit and consume her heart.

She pretended her way through each day. At dawn Payton was away on an overnight business trip, although he had never taken one before. At lunch he couldn't meet her because he had to attend a seminar. Through the long evening he was working late. As she surrendered to exhaustion and sleep mercifully interred her soul, Gloria convinced herself that Payton would join her before morning. When he wasn't there to silence the alarm, she began the cycle once more.

"Hi, Glor-ya! I brung you something!"

Seven-year-old Cassie Carter smiled brilliantly up at Gloria over the top of a cardboard box. *Glow little glow worm, shine and...* Gloria held the door open wide so the child could maneuver her burden inside.

Cassie carefully placed the box on the sofa and arranged herself beside it. Gloria watched her and felt tears threatening yet again. She cried every day over one thing or another. *But not in front of Cassie...*

She and Payton had tried to have a baby, but one or maybe both of them were incapable of generating a pregnancy. They never discovered the cause of their infertility, and neither of them cared. They had each other, and their love was blessing enough.

Cassie had been an infant when Gloria and Payton moved to

the neighborhood. They babysat her often, and she adopted them as a second set of parents. Payton adored her, and Cassie thought he hung the moon, but only because her own daddy surely set the sun in the sky.

"Guess what, Glor-ya! Samantha's kittens are ten weeks old today! Daddy says I can keep one, but I have to give the rest away."

Gloria eyed the cardboard box nervously. "I'm sure you'll find nice homes for them, honey," she offered.

"I already found a home for one!" Cassie proclaimed proudly. She dove into the box with both hands and emerged with a misty tuft of fur that she eagerly thrust at Gloria.

A pair of emerald moons regarded her earnestly for all of two seconds.

"Eeeeeeooow!" he objected, and squirmed frantically in Cassie's grip.

Gloria agreed. But when Cassie cried, "Ouch, take him!" Gloria had no choice but to detach the kitten from Cassie's shirt and place him on her own lap.

"I picked him out especially for you!" Cassie smiled happily. "I know you must get lonesome here all by yourself. And I know you really miss Uncle Payt. We all do! So you need a friend who will keep you company and listen when you need somebody to talk to. And he needs somebody to play with him and take care of him." She reached over and petted the kitten, who poised for flight from Gloria's lap. "So you're perfect for each other!"

Gloria struggled for words that would return the gift without breaking the giver's heart. "Cassie, I appreciate your thoughtfulness and concern, I really do, but I just don't think I can give him the…" She choked on the word. "…the love he needs."

"That's okay!" Cassie had it all worked out. "He'll come to you when he wants attention! That's why I picked him for you. He's the biggest of the whole litter, and he was the first one to get out of the basket and run all over the house, and he bosses the other kittens around. I was gonna keep him myself, but you need him more than I do. Just let him love you until he gives you so much love that you have enough to give some back!" She jumped off the couch. "I brung you some more stuff, too! Come see!"

Cassie tugged on Gloria's wrist. The kitten saw his chance to launch off her leg and flee to parts unknown. Gloria sighed helplessly and allowed Cassie to tow her out the door.

A little red wagon waited on the sidewalk. Cassie had stocked it with a bag of cat litter, a box of kitten food, a basket lined with a flannel cushion, and a catnip toy.

"You'll need a container for this," Cassie pointed at the bag. "An old cake pan will do until you can buy a litter box. Be sure and leave fresh water for him all the time," she continued with a professional air. "And play with him a lot! He loves to chase things. Daddy says he's really aggressive, whatever that means."

She chattered on about the cats and her Daddy and Uncle Payt, and what else could Gloria do? When the wagon had been unloaded and Cassie was ready to go home, Gloria lifted the child in her arms and held her, held her tight...

Life was a broad spectrum of recurring cycles, she thought, pondering the miniature philosopher who had revealed so much in so few words. She pulled a frightened, hissing fur tuft from a shoe box in the hall closet and sang it to sleep in her lap, strangely comforted by the tiny tom kitten who was born the day her husband died.

She named the kitten Socrates. And though she had forgotten how to smile, vainly forbidden herself to cry, and quelled any other emotion that threatened to make her feel, Socrates marched right into her home and her heart and promptly established ownership of both.

Gloria sank ever deeper into the growing abyss of depression. She had not filled the absence of her married friends by finding single ones, and her parents had their own lives to live. She had no desire to go out alone. She had not prayed since the day her husband died, feeling cut off even from God. Her only friend, indeed, was Socrates. He presented himself a sympathetic offering to hold and hug as needed, quietly sharing her sorrow, patiently licking her tears from his coat. He gave her unconditional love, hilarious entertainment, and the routine responsibility of care and feeding. He became the only constant in a life in turmoil.

Five months after Payton's death, Gloria faced their tenth wedding anniversary alone. She called in sick to work that morning, then went anyway, then came home early and begged God, if He was listening, to come and get her, too.

Late that evening she went for a walk. Autumn tinged the trees with color and the air breathed crisp and cool. Gloria barely noticed the seasons changing around her. Grief had stripped her life of its beauty like winter would soon strip the trees of theirs.

"Hi, Glor-ya! How's Socrates! Can we go with you?" Gloria exchanged brief pleasantries with Cassie's parents. They lagged respectfully behind as Gloria continued her solitary walk, but Cassie bounced alongside her, chattering constantly, and suddenly they were at the park across the street from the church. Gloria hadn't meant to come this far. *Oh, God, don't make me look over there...*

"Look!" Cassie pointed to the heavens. "See that star up there? Not the great big one – the little one that's barely shining, right next to it. You have to look real hard to see it."

Gloria studied the millions of radiant planets strewn across the firmament until she focused on the one she believed Cassie wanted her to see.

"That," Cassie announced softly, "is the Spencer star. I picked it out myself when me and Daddy were looking through our telescope, and I named it after you and Uncle Payt."

Gloria looked at the barely discernible pinprick of light and responded moodily. "Why such a little, insignificant star? Why not the big bright one next to it?"

"Because it won't be around much longer," Cassie replied. "Daddy says there's a legend that stars twinkle the most and shine the brightest right before they die. And you and Payton will love each other forever, even if he's in Heaven and you're here, and so I wanted to pick a star for you that will last almost that long."

Gloria smiled at Cassie, even as the tears came. She stared up at the minute star, and as she wept it began to dance and glimmer and glisten through the tears that distorted her vision, and suddenly she knew – she knew! – the answer to her lifelong question, as simple and eloquent and precious and rare as sun shining through pouring rain, as a smile of newborn hope flickering through tears of heart-wrenching sorrow, as laughter over fond memories balancing the empty regret of loss.

Cassie began to cry, too, until Gloria hugged her and kissed her and thanked her for her beautiful gift. "I'm going to sit here for a while and watch our star," she said, and that made Cassie happy, and she trotted away to join her parents on their walk back home.

Gloria sat on a park bench and laughed and cried and watched the star. Truths she had heard all her life began to sink in, words of advice and encouragement, psalms of tragedy and of triumph. Reality came to visit, bringing wisdom she hadn't been able to comprehend before.

Of course everything she did was somehow connected to Payton. That's what happens when the two become one. That is how it's supposed to be. And grieving was natural and a part of her always would. But her tribute to Payton should be one of joy and not of sorrow, for he had surely been the best husband in the world, had made her the happiest wife, would have laid down his life before he would have caused her to cry. If she had known exactly how it was going to end and how badly it was going to hurt, Gloria knew that she still would have married Payton and done everything exactly as they had, because she wouldn't have missed the love they shared for anything in the world.

And she began to pray.

Thank you for the seven-year-old child who saw the space and time in my life from a different point of view and offered solutions and suggestions to fill both.

Thank you for Socrates and his wisdom and perception that are often far above my own.

Thank you for my daddy and Cassie's daddy and all the

daddies in the world who take the time to be real fathers to their little girls and boys.

Thank you most of all for Payton, for my beloved husband, the greatest gift you have ever given me, second only to my own salvation. Thank you for his unconditional, never-ending love, for the man he was and the woman he taught me to be. Thank you for the time we had together and for the reassurance that we'll be together again.

Gloria remembered and laughed and cried for hours into the night.

And she watched the star until it dropped out of sight just beyond the crest of the hill.

On This Wise

A work of fiction based on Matthew 2:1-12

Covington : December 2017

"Because it's a myth!" Holly's tone indicated that she had expected her companions to know this.

"That's sacrilege, child." Nana rose from the piano and left the room.

"Are you happy now? You've hurt Ma's feelings." Grace fixed her daughter with the darkest expression she could muster, which wasn't especially intimidating on a woman holding a flocked camel under each arm. "Just once in a while, I wish you'd trade your know-it-all attitude for a moment of mature consideration. Your so-called myth is sacred truth to a lot of people."

"But the truth is exactly what I'm talking about," Holly insisted, unwrapping an Oriental figure in elaborate costume. "Read the Bible for yourself, Mom. These guys weren't kings, they weren't from the Orient, and nowhere is it written that there were only three. They were wise men from the east, whatever that means."

"It means Christmas, Holly. Go apologize to your grandmother. And see that you don't upset anyone else with your urge to correct their beliefs."

Holly sighed in exasperation as she placed the figure on the floor beside its camel.

❊ ❊ ❊ ❊ ❊

Syria, northeast of Damascus : January : 3 B.C.

Melchar pulled the linen robe snug around his neck, reluctant to cover his head despite the cold, misting rain. He envied the laborers in their woolen clothing: unadorned, signifying their caste, but warmer than the richly dyed cloth reserved for the royal priesthood. It was pointless, this deliberate exposure to the elements. The sky was overcast and the Star, though it could vaguely be discerned, would soon vanish with the dawn.

He clutched to his chest the parchments on which he had carefully charted the celestial phenomenon they had pursued for months. No less than a dozen Median priests were scattered about squinting toward the heavens as they studied Mithraic prophecies on scrolls, drew astrological maps, and recorded their own accounts of the event. Behind them, amidst the clatter of a caravan settling for a day of rest, a singular noise penetrated Melchar's own study, persistently alerting him that a once-small problem was growing steadily critical. With a farewell glance to his elusive quarry, he hurried into the camp.

A tent had been erected, before which a fire warmly blazed. Beltazaar crouched against the flame, trembling with fever, rendered breathless and weak by an incessant cough. He opened his eyes when Melchar clasped under his arms and drew him into the tent.

"How does it look for me now?" His voice was little more than a whisper.

Melchar had hoped the question would not arise, for he could not lie to a friend and an elder. He solemnly met Beltazaar's rheumy gaze, and the old man nodded in resignation.

"So be it as the stars have said," he murmured. "So be it, but for one request. I desire that my eyes might behold the fulfillment of the prophecy before I am gathered to my fathers. Can you cling to my life for me, Melchar, until then?"

Melchar drew a robe around Beltazaar's narrow shoulders. "I will prepare the tea."

All the medicines in the world would not prevent the inevitable. Melchar had consulted the constellations, prescribed herbs, applied poultices to Beltazaar's throat and chest until the old man's hide peeled in protest. Melchar could bring about relief of aching stiffness in old joints, comfort against digestive disturbances, a cure for sleepless nights, but this particular illness defied his medical expertise. Progression would slow, whether out of generosity or mockery Melchar could not tell, and then bear down again, brutally pressing life out of Beltazaar's frail body. Age was a traitor equal to the malady, formidable foes sharing a pact against the ancient magus. There was little Melchar could do in retribution.

Beltazaar talked while Melchar brewed the tea, alternately reciting liturgies and rambling incoherently about the battle between Ormazd and Ahriman as though it were taking place right in front of him.

Or within him, Melchar thought.

"*Amesha Spenta!*" Beltazaar abruptly proclaimed, staring wide-eyed at the canopy overhead.

Bountiful immortal. Melchar wondered at the pronouncement as he cradled Beltazaar's head and poured the tea between his lips. The sedative effect was almost immediate. Melchar brought out a *Khordah*, recorded by his own hand, and read prayers to Beltazaar until the old man fell into exhausted slumber.

Covington : December 2017

"Happy Birthday to me!" Holly prowled like a cat among the gifts beneath the tree. "Well, almost. Don't suppose I could open one a day early?"

Grace smiled at her own Christmas child. She wished she had not been so quick to dismiss her daughter's inquisitive nature. She whispered a prayer for forgiveness. "Sure, Holly. Which one would you like?"

"Thanks, Mom." Holly lifted a small box tied with gold ribbon. "I'm sorry for my comments about the music. I didn't mean any offense. I find the 'three kings' song a little frustrating. That song and these guys." She straightened the robe of a bearded king. "The story is a legend based on assumption."

Grace shrugged. "A lot of Christmas traditions are variations of customs that have been passed down through history. Except for the accounts of Jesus' birth that we read in the Bible, more holiday celebrations are rooted in legend than in reality. That shouldn't stop you from enjoying them."

Holly spiraled the ribbon around her finger. "But the magi, Mom. Think about it. However many of whatever they were, they followed a star they'd never seen before based on a prophecy that was centuries old, in hopes that the star would lead them to a supernatural king. I suppose if the song is fiction, it's no stranger than the few facts that we do know."

"The magi existed, or they wouldn't have been mentioned in the Bible," Grace said.

"Oh, I'm sure the wise men were real. I have no trouble believing that. I just wish we could know who they really were."

Grace sat on the floor beside her daughter. "So do I." She tugged mischievously at the gift in Holly's hands. "Happy sweet sixteen."

✳ ✳ ✳ ✳ ✳

Israel, north of Jerusalem : January : 3 B.C.

Melchar clenched his teeth and urged his mount onward. He rode a fine horse, an intelligent steed that responded well to discipline. The animal's good nature and sensibilities were tasked to the limit, however, by the presence of a camel on a lead.

Beltazaar had insisted he was strong enough to ride without assistance, so Melchar reluctantly resumed his usual place near the front of the caravan for the darkening hours following the sunset. After the moon peaked and began her descent toward the horizon, he heard Beltazaar coughing more frequently and noticed that he leaned unsteadily forward in his saddle. Melchar moved back to lead Beltazaar's mount for the remainder of the night.

"How is he?" Darek drew his horse alongside Melchar. "He looks bad."

"He is weak and tired," Melchar responded, carefully impassive. "He is sick."

Darek gazed for a moment at the Star and turned to Melchar, stricken. "Beltazaar has been a father to me, a mentor. He always has an answer to my question. Who will answer my question when Beltazaar is no longer among us?"

"A place of rest awaits him until Ahura Mazda triumphs over Angra Mainyu and welcomes the virtuous souls into his kingdom," Melchar reminded him. "Meditate upon the scriptures and take comfort in knowing that you will see Beltazaar again in the afterlife."

The words did not help, but both pretended otherwise. Darek pulled ahead in the caravan, leaving Melchar alone with his own hopeless wishes. He distracted himself from Beltazaar's condition by focusing on the guiding Star and contemplating the prophecies by which the magi pursued this alien light.

The people of Judah had been carried away captive into Babylon half a millennium ago. When Cyrus ascended to the Persian throne some five decades later, he promptly conquered the Medes and proceeded to take Lydia and Babylon, thereby inheriting the captive Jews. One year after that, Cyrus issued a decree permitting the captives to return to Palestine and rebuild their temple. However, many of the Jews chose life under Persian rule over the opportunity, and the burden, of restoring Jerusalem. Their descendants held faithfully to ancestral custom and, as a result, the Jewish prophecies were as well known among the magi as their own Zoroastrian scriptures. Both religious studies predicted that a new star would herald the arrival of a supernatural messiah of royal birth.

The brilliant entity the magi followed had appeared one evening without preamble, gloriously radiating beams to the horizon. The magi – astrologers, magicians, priests – gazed in awe at this new light awakened in the heavens. Every day thereafter they pondered ancient prophecies, and every night they sought the sky for answers to questions they feared to ask. Each dusk the Star reappeared to the consternation of some and the delight of all, for it proved not a stationary planet, but a light that traveled without the constraints of orbit, independent of the boundaries of the constellations that ruled the solar system. It was a miracle. It was a wonder. It was an invitation to come and discover if the prophecies were true. Twelve months from the Star's first appearing, a caravan set out westward across the desert, uncertain how far away in time and distance the assumed Prince might be found. The Median priests had pursued their Sign faithfully every night thereafter.

A ripple of unrest began at the head of the caravan, the leaders slowing and pointing straight ahead as they looked to the sky. By the time Darek rode back to Melchar, the entire procession had halted. Darek answered before Melchar asked.

"The Star no longer appears to be moving." His breath caught in his throat with excitement. "We must have achieved our glorious destination! In the morning we will enter Jerusalem and inquire of Herod the King as to whether we may gain audience with the child Prince."

✵ ✵ ✵ ✵ ✵

Jerusalem : January : 3 B.C.

Their entrance into the city was met with eyes wide and jaws agape, this contingent of a royal priesthood who had traveled more than one thousand miles in the wake of a Star that, it was foretold, would lead them to a god-king. Deity or not, it was in the best interest of politics to welcome the Prince into the world with due benevolence. It was never too soon to nurture good relations between ruling entities. Thus they rode into Jerusalem on carefully groomed and costumed horses, Median astrologers dressed in their finest apparel, mistaken by many to be exotic kings and foreign rulers on the mere basis of first impression.

Seven magi presented themselves to Herod, who received them with ill-concealed trepidation. Melchar was of necessity among them, for he alone was fluent in the native dialects. Introductions were barely accomplished before Herod inquired as to the purpose of their visit.

"We have come to pay homage to the King whose birth was announced by the Star of prophecy."

Herod blinked without expression, but his face slowly turned crimson as he cogitated on the implications of Melchar's answer. As the revelation sank in, Herod called forth a weak smile and a number of priests from the local temple to explain what such prophesies could possibly have to do with Jerusalem.

Nothing, Herod's priests informed him. According to the prophet Micah, this Jewish messiah, the King of the Jews, would be born in Bethlehem of Judæa. A sign of the birth would indeed be the appearance of a brilliant new star in the heavens.

"A Jewish King." Herod arose from his throne and descended the dais. He strolled away from the magi, then turned abruptly to face them. "When did this Star first appear to announce the child's birth?"

Melchar distrusted the emotions that twisted Herod's features with amusement, rage, and fear. He reluctantly answered. "About sixteen months ago."

Herod nodded thoughtfully. "I must also pay homage to this King. Go and seek him out. When you have found him, bring me word again, that I might visit the divine offspring and serve him with appropriate respect."

Covington : December 2017

Holly lifted the necklace by its chain and stared as it glistened in the light. "What does it say on the back? 'With all our love.' Are you sure you want to part with it?"

"My mother and father gave this locket to me on my sixteenth birthday," Grace softly replied. "There was a picture of them inside. I left it there for you. Perhaps you'll pass it on to your daughter someday."

"I remember that picture." Nana lowered herself stiffly onto the sofa and nodded at Grace. "I remember posing beside your father while my brother showed off his new camera out at the old home place. My mama gave me that locket on my sixteenth birthday, but there wasn't a picture in it until I gave it to you." She turned to her granddaughter. "And now it's yours, Holly. You remember this occasion. This is how traditions get started."

"I will, Nana," Holly replied, but her gaze drifted again to the nativity set beside the tree.

Grace exhaled an exasperated sigh, but Nana studied the colorful figures approaching the manger and allowed herself to question, just for a moment, how they fit into the Christ child's story.

✳ ✳ ✳ ✳ ✳

Bethlehem : January : 3 B.C.

Beltazaar was, if nothing else, determined. He had rallied from the verge of death yet again, awed as the rest when their caravan crested a hill and looked out across the City of David. Their celestial guide moved no farther. It rested, still and serene and brilliant and unmistakable, above Bethlehem.

Melchar dismounted and reached up to Beltazaar as he commanded the camel to kneel. "We can sleep through the remainder of the night. We will search for the Jewish messiah in the morning."

"No," Beltazaar protested. "We must find him now, while the Star yet shines. His own people do not appear to know him, and we are strangers here. How will we recognize him, when no man can lead us to him, if we have not the Star to guide us?"

The message flowed like water throughout the caravan, and the other magi, whether in agreement with Beltazaar or out of venerable respect, moved the caravan to the outskirts of the city. Leaving laborers to set up their camp, the magi continued into Bethlehem, searching for a place in which the rays of light descending from the Star might meet the earth. Most walked, but Beltazaar remained aboard his camel, and Melchar rode his horse alongside. They hurried as best they could among the narrow streets in search of a destination that might fulfill a world of prophecies. As the night progressed, they divided into companies and searched the whole of Bethlehem, but no place was found of which the Star seemed especially fond. After a dejected consultation, the magi trudged wearily toward the edge of town from whence they had arrived.

And there it was. A small house, plain and unpretentious, with a tiny woodshop attached to one side. It was the last home on the outskirts of town, and they had trotted right past it hours before in their haste to enter the city and locate the King. They stopped before the simple home bathed in Starlight, and Melchar shivered at the sensation that he had entered a presence far greater than that of any ruler he had ever known. He glanced at his contemporaries and found similar emotions expressed on each face. They stared in reverent wonder until Darek broke the silence. He spoke quietly, as though fearful of interrupting the moment.

"We will return after the family has awakened. We should go back to camp now and record the last of the Star's journey and its destination. We need to prepare our gifts for the King."

✳ ✳ ✳ ✳ ✳

Covington : December 2017

"Where are you going? The weather is terrible out there. I can hear sleet against the window." Nana hugged her afghan closer.

"Just down to Deal's." Holly buttoned her coat. "Curfew, I know. I won't be long. There's one more gift I need to get."

"Well, this is a fine time to think of it," Grace said. "I don't like you going out this late on Christmas Eve."

"I'll be careful, Mom, I promise." Holly kissed her mother and her grandmother.

"You've got your scarf and gloves?" Grace asked, and Holly held them up. "And your cell phone?"

"And my key to the front door. Love you!" Holly, with her perpetual enthusiasm and her birthday locket, stepped out into the snow.

✳ ✳ ✳ ✳ ✳

Bethlehem : January : 3 B.C.

Breakfast was accomplished on the merits of convention, prepared and eaten in a vague acceptance that it must be, and therefore was, done. Bethlehem awoke before dawn had fully exchanged her diaphanous nightwear for daytime garb. The city bustled with activity by the time the magi and half the strength of their caravan approached the little house.

Darek would have knocked on the door, had the appearance of a man from the woodshop not spared him the effort. The stout young carpenter, perhaps in his early thirties, gaped in astonishment at the regal entourage before him. Melchar stepped forth and introduced them as the Magi, the priesthood descended from those who served Zarathusthra for the kings of the ancient Median-Persian empire, come to worship the Jewish King whose birth was announced by the strange new Star.

Instead of expressing even greater incredulity at this announcement, the Galilean relaxed as though such a visit were a perfectly normal occurrence and pushed open the door of his house for them. "I am Joseph," he announced simply. "The child and His mother are here. You are welcome in our home."

They entered softly, as though afraid to disturb some holy scene, but were immediately put at ease by the squeal of a young boy scampering through the room, closely pursued by his mother.

"Mary." Joseph nodded in her direction. "My wife. The child you sought is Jesus."

Melchar looked the young mother over with dismay. She was a lovely girl, hardly more than a child, and would not be a woman for years yet to come. He wondered if civilizations would ever advance to the point that fathers would allow their daughters to become women before giving them in marriage on the belief that as soon as a girl began to menstruate she should begin bearing children. It grieved him to see girls not fully grown carrying babies in their bellies, struggling to give birth, often dying in the process.

But this child was fathered by a god, and a god would have had no choice in the matter, Melchar thought, if He wanted His son to be born of a virgin. Even God would have had to select a girl to bear His blessing and fulfill His promise, because social structures rarely permitted young women to complete their teen years unmarried and childless.

His companions interrupted his reverie as they drifted alongside and past him, filling the room and gazing with adoration at the boy in his mother's arms. Melchar looked around their little home, struck by the incongruence of a king born to a carpenter. A king should possess wealth and riches, not only for luxury and comfort, but because financial prosperity was necessary to establish a ruler. How could the boy possibly hope to ascend to any throne from these humble beginnings? Melchar was glad of the gift he had chosen for the child. He stepped forward and lowered a cloth bag to the ground beside Mary's feet, opening it to reveal the gold pieces inside. Her eyes widened with wonder as she sat on a stool beside the gift with her son on her lap.

Others moved forward, then, with gifts of gold, precious stones, fine linens, offerings befitting the grandest of Kings. Melchar smiled in approval. The foundations for prosperity were laid. Melchar wondered what kingdom the child would someday rule.

Darek approached and knelt before the boy with an alabaster box of frankincense, a sweet odor burned throughout the centuries in religious ceremonies by priests offering oblations to their gods. Others came behind Darek with similar gifts, all befitting a member of a royal priesthood.

Melchar's arm was grasped firmly in a trembling grip as old Beltazaar moved past him on his way to Jesus. The elderly man sank heavily to the floor by Mary's feet and held forth a jar. Melchar winced at what it contained even as he understood, in accordance with the Jewish predictions for the child's eventual death, the significance of such a gift. The child gripped the jar of myrrh with both hands as Mary took it from Beltazaar and placed it on a table behind her stool. The boy reached out to Beltazaar, who took the child into his own lap. Beltazaar rocked the child and sobbed, heartbroken, as he recited the prophecies that foretold the death of the man the boy would someday become.

Jesus cuddled against the old man and patted his shoulder, then drew back and playfully grabbed Beltazaar's beard. He pulled down on the beard until he could kiss the wrinkled brown cheek. "*Abba* loves you. *Abba's!*" He pounded a small fist against Beltazaar's chest. "*Mine!*" The boy clapped his hands with exuberance, threw his little arms around Beltazaar's neck, and hugged tightly as though he would never let go, while the old man clung to the child and wept with unspeakable joy.

❋ ❋ ❋ ❋ ❋

Covington : December 2017

Holly hurried along for several blocks before turning toward town. She doubted the store would have the items she wanted, but perhaps she could find a satisfactory substitute that would help her make things right with her grandmother. She slowed as she passed the museum, surprised to see lights on in the rear of the building. She had worked in the gift shop all summer and knew she could find exactly what she wanted there. Of course it was closed on Christmas Eve night, but Holly pulled out her cell phone anyway and scrolled through the index until she found her former employer's number.

"Curator's office," announced a tired male voice.

"Hey, Thomas, this is Holly."

"Holly! How on earth have you been? You haven't stopped by to see us lately. We've missed having you around. But this is an odd time to call. Is everything okay?"

"Everything's fine," Holly assured him. "This is going to sound strange, but I have a favor to ask."

"Name it. I'll be glad to help you in any way I can."

Holly briefly stated her request, and Thomas laughed heartily into the phone.

"That's it? I was afraid you were in some kind of trouble. Come on in. You won't be disturbing me. I'll be here until midnight, anyway. Just knock on the side door. I'll brew some tea."

❋ ❋ ❋ ❋ ❋

Arabian Desert : February : 3 B.C.

"Melchar, awake! Hurry!"

Melchar responded to the panic in Darek's voice by abandoning his bedding for the cool night breeze before he was even coherent. He staggered and almost fell as he muzzily watched Darek sprint away through the camp. Melchar pulled himself together and trotted after the younger man, forcing himself to full consciousness as he ran.

Melchar smelled the stench as he approached the tent. A group of men had already moved Beltazaar out under the open sky and were dismantling his tent in order to burn it. Darek wept, inconsolable.

"We were talking, and he began speaking nonsense," Darek explained. "I could tell he was sick, and I told him I would bring you with your medicines. He called out to the boy Jesus, to the Jewish God, and then he collapsed." Darek raised tear-filled eyes to the sky. "It was the dream that finished him. It was too great a dream for a frail old man. It was more than he could bear!"

Melchar gave orders to wash the body as he returned to his own tent to assemble the spices and fragrances used in embalming. He shuddered at the memory of that night in Bethlehem. After a day spend in the presence of Joseph and Mary and the child King Jesus, the magi and their attendants had collapsed into a grateful sleep in their camp outside the city. Beltazaar experienced a violent dream that night, a visitation from the God of Israel who instructed him that the magi should return to their homeland via a different route because King Herod meant to take their lives and the life of the child they had traveled so far to see.

Melchar wanted to share this dream with Joseph and encourage him to join the magi with his family in order to escape Herod's intentions. Beltazaar shocked everyone by refusing to alert Joseph to the danger, insisting that the same God who had spoken to him in a dream would speak to Joseph as well in order to spare the child's life. They had broken camp immediately and set out northeast before daybreak, skirting the Dead Sea and hurrying eastward across Jordan.

They were now in the middle of the Arabian desert, miles from cities and civilizations, and Melchar had no spices with which to embalm the man who had been to him, also, a priest, a father, a mentor. He enquired throughout the company for herbs, frankincense, myrrh, anything he might use to prepare Beltazaar for a proper burial, but none were to be found. All such possessions had been left behind in Bethlehem, gifted to the child King.

Melchar raged, he wept, he beseeched the constellations for

those things he so desperately needed. In the end, he prepared the fragile old body in accordance with custom, removing the vital internal organs and placing them in jars, cleansing the abdominal cavity and filling it with sand in lieu of the aromatic spices that should have sweetened the precious, deceased body. He wrapped Beltazaar tightly in strips of clean cloth and watched in helpless despair as laborers buried his beloved friend under the desert sands.

❋ ❋ ❋ ❋ ❋

Covington : December 2017

Thomas greeted Holly with an enthusiastic hug, sat her in front of a heater, and shoved a porcelain teacup in her hand. Holly inhaled the warm fragrance of cinnamon as she sipped from the tiny cup, placed it gingerly onto its saucer, and settled the delicate affair onto the table beside her chair.

"In a hurry?" Thomas asked. "Of course, you would be. Look at the time, both the hour and the day! I haven't much family with whom to celebrate, and so I forget to show proper respect for the schedules of those who do. Please forgive me." He led Holly into the museum, through a labyrinth of corridors to the gift shop. He produced a ring bristling with keys, selected one without even looking, and unlocked the door.

Holly went straight to a display of imported containers and selected a small alabaster jar approximately two inches tall. She hurried to another display and then to a cabinet along one wall before meeting Thomas at the cash register with her selections.

"That's it? These are all you wanted? You may have them, Holly. No, I won't accept payment. Ah, blasted telephone. I'd better take this call. Have a Merry Christmas, Holly. Give Grace my regards."

Holly made her way through the dark halls back to the office. She paused for one more sip of tea from the dainty cup, pulled on her gloves, and headed home.

✳ ✳ ✳ ✳ ✳

Persia : January : 2 B.C.

Though cluttered with the usual array of constellations, the sky spread vast and empty without the Star. Melchar missed the Star not only in the heavens, but also in his heart. Both felt vacant in the absence of that light. In the months since his return from Bethlehem, Melchar had addressed his inability to rest with every conceivable resolution. On this night, the second anniversary of the Star's first appearance, he finally confessed that he suffered from an insatiable spiritual hunger. All his knowledge could not settle his mind. His wealth could not purchase a balm to soothe his hurt. Food and drink could not fill his need. No relationship with another person could cure this heartsickness that ached at the very core of his being. Though physically healthy, he felt hollow, burned of a fever, and he yearned desperately for this nameless longing to be filled.

His young friend Darek had prayed to the God of the Jews in the name of the child Jesus since the day they laid Beltazaar to rest in the desert. Beltazaar had known this God, and that was proof enough for Darek of His existence. Darek insisted that God heard his prayers and responded to them. Was that the answer? *Yahweh ... Jehovah ... are You the Answer?* As Melchar stared into the sky at the constellations he knew so well, his soul searched beyond the stars, reaching out to the Creator of them all.

✳ ✳ ✳ ✳ ✳

Covington : December 2017

"She's back, Grace," Nana called from the sofa. "Your mother was certain you'd catch your death out there," she informed Holly.

"Not that you ever entertained such thoughts about me when I was her age," Grace said.

"You're dripping," Nana complained. "At least stand on the

rug."

Holly complied as she peeled off her coat and stepped out of her wet shoes.

"No luck?" Grace asked.

Holly dug into her pocket and pulled out a small bag. "Who is it for?" Nana wanted to know.

"They are gifts for our crèche." Holly knelt beside the figures on the floor and stuffed the little alabaster jar into the saddlebag of the camel that belonged to the Ethiopian King.

"What is it, and why, if you don't mind?"

Holly smiled at Grace. "It is supposed to be myrrh. Tradition has it that this king, Balthasar, offered myrrh to the Christ child. Gaspar offered frankincense, and Melchoir offered gold." She arranged a small porcelain box in the hands of the second king, and placed a miniature carved chest on the floor beside the third. "Myrrh was special. It was a product that a wealthy man of that period would store away for his own death to guarantee proper embalming and burial. Frankincense was also a precious gift. Chances are that if Balthasar and Gaspar presented myrrh and frankincense to Jesus, they were giving their own supply away. I noticed that the three kings were here with their camels, but they had no gifts for Jesus. I thought I'd supply them – in keeping with tradition." She took off her heart-shaped locket and lowered it carefully into Melchoir's wooden chest. "Since I don't have anything else that's real gold," Holly said, "I'll let them borrow my birthday gift for a couple of days."

"Does this mean you've changed your mind about the song?" Nana asked hopefully.

"No. It just means I've made up my own mind about the magi."

"And what have you decided?" Grace joined Nana on the sofa.

"I believe that what the Bible says is true. The magi were searching for something beyond their understanding. They recognized Jesus as the answer when they found Him. They allowed their knowledge to confirm their faith, instead of using it as a weapon to rationalize away their conviction. Whatever else they might have been, they were indeed very wise men. Go ahead and sing the song, Nana. But can we skip the first verse?"

Nana returned to the piano and began to sing. *Born a babe on Bethlehem's plain; gold we bring to crown Him again...*

Holly and her mother sang the last verse together. *Glorious now, behold Him arise: King and God and Sacrifice...*

"Merry Christmas, Nana." Holly smiled at the crèche. "Merry Christmas, Mom."

Nana and Grace echoed the sentiment, and then stopped to listen to carolers outside the front door.

"Hark, the herald angels sing..."

"You know, Matthew was the only disciple who wrote about the journey of the magi," Holly said. "The physician Luke records the angels' visitation to the shepherds, but he says nothing about the heavenly host breaking into song."

"Holly," Grace warned.

"But maybe they did," Nana said, "and Luke just didn't make note of it. He had quite a story to tell, after all. It would have been impossible for him to include every single detail."

"That's true," Holly conceded. "But on this subject, I really do wish I knew it all."

The room came alive with laughter as three generations of women joined hands and sang along with the carolers.

Hark, the herald angels sing! Glory to the newborn King!

Heaven

Beyond what we call mystical,
Farther than planet seeds are sown,
Lies someplace more than mythical,
That mortal minds have never known.

Those who now sleep in Paradise
Will be awakened by a glance
From all creation's Father's eyes
As Life performs her final dance.

See them fly with Spirit wings,
Those who their final grief have shed;
Where once a voiceless soul, now sings
With triumph, in that Death is dead.

Within a blink, those who remain,
And who laid claim to Sacrifice,
Release from bond of mortal chain
That which was bought with priceless Price.

No more desire for things before;
What has now past we comprehend
As nothing lost, for through the Door
Are love and life that have no end.

Love fulfills Hope, Faith becomes sight,
And past the hallowed judgment halls
We ever view by raptured light
A place where darkness never falls.

Beyond what we call mystical,
More beautiful than earth could stand,
Lies somewhere more than mythical:
A blest, eternal, Promised Land.

*To everyone
who has joined
me on the
journey:
this adventure
is dedicated
to you.*

ACTownsend

has spent a lifetime writing fiction and nonfiction. She earned a degree in Criminal Justice and has worked as an emergency services photographer. Her talent for conducting interviews and research led to a successful career as a reporter for a local newspaper and as a feature writer for an area magazine. Her first novel, *Journey of The Dead ~ Book One of The Trinity Conspiracy* series, was published in 2014. Townsend lives in Kentucky with her husband and a host of feline muses for whom she maintains a blog at MEOW ~ Melody's Extra Ordinary World.

actownsend.com

www.facebook.com/JoinTheConspiracy

actownsend.com/melodyblog/

Look for A.C. Townsend's novels at Amazon.com, Barnes & Noble online, and Goodreads. If you enjoy an author's book, please leave a review and share your encouragement with other readers!